THE
CROSS
GARDENER

**Center Point
Large Print**

Also by Jason F. Wright
and available from Center Point Large Print:

The Wednesday Letters

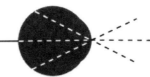

**This Large Print Book carries the
Seal of Approval of N.A.V.H.**

THE
CROSS
GARDENER

Jason F. Wright

CENTER POINT PUBLISHING
THORNDIKE, MAINE

The text of this Large Print edition is unabridged.
In other aspects, this book may vary
from the original edition.
Printed in the United States of America
on permanent paper.
Set in 16-point Times New Roman type.

ISBN: 978-1-60285-759-9

Library of Congress Cataloging-in-Publication Data

Wright, Jason F.
  The cross gardener / Jason F. Wright.
    p. cm.
  ISBN 978-1-60285-759-9 (library binding : alk. paper)
  1. Traffic accident victims--Fiction. 2. Grief--Fiction. 3. Psychological fiction.
  4. Large type books. I. Title.
  PS3623.R539C76 2010b
  813'.6--dc22
2009052535

To my father,
whom I pray will one day be
my own Cross Gardener.

ACKNOWLEDGMENTS

My thanks to Kodi, my wife and best friend, for once again believing. Also to my children: Oakli, Jadi, Kason, and Koleson for keeping Mom sane while I travel.

Eternal appreciation to Dad, Mom, Beverly, Del, Milo, Gayle, Sterling, Ann, Jeff, April, John, Terilynne, and the army of nieces and nephews who give my life the distinct flavor of crazy.

I'm especially grateful to Glaize Orchards in Strasburg, Virginia, and to Tracy, Laura, Michael, Kayla, and Cami Armstrong for teaching me every-thing I needed to know—and more—about apples. The novel wouldn't have ripened without you.

The family of early manuscript readers was more helpful than ever. Huge thanks to Cherie Call Anderson, Matilda Birch, Laurel Christensen, Ally Condie, Stuart and Katie Freakley, Chrissy Funk, Angela Godfrey, Donovan and Susan Marsh, Kevin Milne, Jennifer Oringdulph, Laurie Paisley, Kalley Richardson, Bob and Michelle Rimel, and Kerri Caren Toloczko.

Thank you to old friends who continue to believe and to whom I owe more than I could ever afford to repay in this life or the next: Chris and Kevin Balfe, Glenn Beck, Sheri Dew, and Chris Schoebinger.

Finally, humble thanks to Leslie Gelbman, Sandra Harding, Laurie Liss, and Susan Allison for supporting this author, his novels, and their messages.

One

The Orphan

I was born on the side of a two-lane Virginia highway at 1:21 A.M. on February 1, 1983.

Sixteen years later on my birthday, just as he promised, Father gave me a thick manila envelope holding detailed police, paramedic, and investigative reports. Also included were transcripts from several interviews by a detective who perhaps cared more than he needed to.

Most of the documents were cold and sterile.

Some were revealing.

My mother's name was Libby Riffey, seventeen years old. A resident of Forest Pond Court in Centreville, Virginia. She'd been a ward of the Commonwealth until winning emancipation at age sixteen. That same day she accepted a long-awaited invitation to move in with her best friend, Christa Abbott, and her charismatic, divorced father, Ken.

The girls were inseparable.

Christa taught Libby to love ballet. The two took classes that Ken happily paid for at a prestigious dance studio in Fairfax. Libby had found a mentor there, a woman who believed she could one day dance professionally. Libby was crushed when her hero was diagnosed and killed by breast cancer in just ten months.

Christa taught Libby to deal with sorrow.

Libby taught Christa to stand up for herself at school.

Christa taught Libby to wear makeup and flirt.

Libby taught Christa how to navigate the Metro system in downtown Washington, D.C.

Christa's father loved both girls, but his affection for Libby was different. Just eighteen months after moving in, Libby was nine months pregnant and looking for a way out. Some suspected, but at the time only Libby and Ken knew with certainty the baby was his.

Only Libby cared.

At thirty-nine weeks she took her 1976 Ford Pinto for a Sunday evening drive. The investigator speculated that the young woman probably drove south on 29, then west on 66 past the battlefields of Manassas and the undeveloped fields of Gainesville. A light rain began to fall as she drove farther west.

The report noted that drizzle had likely turned to freezing rain by the time Libby neared the end of 66 and turned south onto 81 into the Shenandoah Valley. She'd taken Exit 298 in Strasburg to Route 11 and turned left, presumably looking to refuel and turn around. But long before she reached a gas station, Libby lost control and the deteriorating road conditions sent her spinning toward the centerline.

She collided head-on with a semitruck carrying leather couches and love seats from North Carolina.

The accident was *weather related* and attributable to *unsafe speeds given the conditions*, the report concluded.

I used to wonder where exactly the collision occurred. Had people said a quiet prayer the next morning when they passed the skid marks and remaining shards of glass too small for the VDOT brooms?

I wondered, too, what my mother saw when the bright lights blinded her. Was she reunited with the ballet instructor she must have still grieved for? Did they dance a familiar routine together?

Perhaps the final seconds were pancaked into one like the hood of her white Pinto. Or did they pass slowly, like those long, uncomfortable closing moments in church when I used to watch the clock from a back pew, waiting for the closing hymn and prayer to end, awaiting all the joy and excitement that called me to the creek at the property line.

Did she find herself weak and afraid, wishing she'd stayed home?

Did she have time to pray?

Did she think of me wriggling in her belly?

Did she see the face of the horrified driver?

Did she see the face of God?

A signed statement said every agency within

fifteen miles responded: Virginia State Police, the Shenandoah Valley Rescue Squad, Strasburg Volunteer Fire Department, and even the town of Toms Brook. But by the time the first trucks arrived, two motorists had already removed Libby from the ravaged, enflamed Pinto. A third man was performing CPR while yet another ran vehicle-to-vehicle looking for blankets.

Three paramedics took over and checked vitals. Libby was in labor and, according to their best judgment, couldn't be transported or even moved to the ambulance without serious risk to mother or baby.

Moments later I was born on the left shoulder of Route 11, approximately a quarter-mile from the exit ramp to Interstate 81, with a dozen strangers watching in the freezing rain. No doubt others watched from the warmth of their cars.

While I was treated in one ambulance, Mother was loaded into another. Both raced north on 81 to the hospital in Winchester, their sirens screaming and lights flashing, radios buzzing with arrival times and protocols. But even I must have known Mother was dead long before they ever left the crash site.

An officer collected items from the glove box and backseat, but an undated note scribbled at the top of a canary copy of a sixteen-year-old police report said that the items were soon "misplaced or inadvertently discarded." Never to be seen again were a map; a purse containing a half package of Trident; a birthday card; a wallet with pictures of my mother and Christa, and her ballet instructor; and a gym bag containing a leotard, two pairs of tattered pink ballet shoes, and an overdue library book: *Baryshnikov in Color* by Mikhail Baryshnikov.

The last item on the report had been found dangling on a silver chain from the rearview mirror: a wooden, keychain-sized white cross.

Two
Sirens

I have always loved the sound of sirens.

When I was five my father picked me up from preschool in the basement of the Presbyterian Church and, because I asked, agreed to take the long way back to his pickup truck. *The long way.* I cannot recall a single time that my father said no to the long way.

The long way. Especially now, years after Father took his own long way Home, the words matter.

Father and I walked past the old Woodstock, Virginia, firehouse most Mondays, Wednesdays, and Fridays that spring. Yes, it *was* old, but not because I was a kid more enamored with fire trucks than architecture. It was old because Father said so; he remembered walking past it when he was a boy and the Ben Franklin Five-and-Dime was still on the corner of Court and Main Street.

My busy-boy mind cheered when Father was too late to register me for the other preschool just a few miles from the orchard we lived on near Route 55 in Strasburg. That preschool looked nice when we visited, and it had the extra-high metal slide with the two bumps that if you went fast enough you could catch air on the second one, but it wasn't anywhere near their town's firehouse. And besides, I doubted the Strasburg firehouse could possibly be as old as the one on Court Street.

The three women who ran the other preschool twenty minutes away in Woodstock said they would be *thrilled* to have me, even though we showed up two weeks into the school year. I didn't know what it meant to be *thrilled*; I only knew they made me feel safe the three days a week I ventured off the sanctity of the orchard.

"You want to walk the long way? Again? And what have you done to deserve taking the long way?" Father took my hand and led me westward on Court Street in the opposite direction of his truck.

I didn't answer because the routine didn't require it. Instead I squeezed his hand three times, giving the Wayne Bevan family signal for *I love you.*

He squeezed mine back four times. *I love you, too.*

I looked up at him. In moments like those he seemed to tower taller than even the tallest trees on our fifty-three-acre apple orchard.

"John, I will never say no to the long way." He said the words without a smile on his face. I didn't mind that he didn't smile much with his mouth. He smiled with words.

My senses stood up when we crossed Main Street, passed the jail, and approached the fire-house. There were six enormous white doors. The first two, built in 1930 according to a special stone placed in the brick wall, kept a pair of antique fire trucks safe from vandals and the elements. The middle two doors, built during the expansion of 1961, held two newer fire trucks. But the last two doors held the newest shiny trucks with the bold flat fronts.

They began to open and an innocent bell sounded.

I ripped free from Father's grasp and ran toward the gap where I just knew I'd see a fire truck freed of the reflections in the wavy glass windows. I was stopped from behind just as I arrived at the fire truck's path. Father grabbed the back of my blue fabric belt with one hand and placed the other strongly across my chest, like a thick, taut seat belt at impact. His bony fingers stretched completely across to the ends of my ribs.

Before I could protest, a chorus of angry sirens and horns jumped through the air. I jumped, too, right into my father's arms. I covered my ears and Father backed us away while the fire engine roared out of the station. It turned right onto Main and punched its impatient siren twice more.

Father carried me another block in our well-worn path back to the truck. It took nearly that long for my ears to stop ringing.

"Are you alright, John?"

"Uh-huh."

He set me down on my feet.

"Do I need to tell you what you did wrong?"

I should have answered faster.

"John Bevan, are you *listening*?"

"Yes, sir."

"Do I need to tell you what you did wrong?"

"No, sir."

"That was loud, wasn't it?"

"Yes, sir."

"You know why they blast those sirens and horns?"

I knew, but I also knew he'd tell me anyway.

"They're warnings, John. Warnings to stay away and warnings to make room."

I nodded.

"You ever been that close when one was tearing off like that?"

"No, sir."

"Well, John, they're a different sort of beast when they're on duty, aren't they?"

"Yes, sir." I jammed my index fingers into my ears and wiggled them. "My ears still sound funny."

"That's normal, John." He took my hand and we finished the long circular walk back to his truck parked by the Presbyterian Church. After buckling in and starting the engine, Father put his hand on my knee and said, "Some things are better appreciated from a distance, aren't they, John? Those beautiful rigs are fun to see parked in their firehouse, but when there's work to be done, we let them do it and stand clear, understood?"

I nodded, even though I hadn't heard everything he'd said.

"You're a good boy, John Bevan."

Normally I would have smiled, maybe even said thank you. But this time I was too busy thinking of my mother.

Had she loved sirens, too?

Three
The Orchard

I was four when I first saw the orchard.

It wasn't meant to be permanent. I'd been in three foster homes already, but for "reasons beyond the parents' control," said the pretty caseworker with strong perfume and white tennis shoes on her feet, "things have not gone as agreed."

"I understand," Wayne Bevan said.

"It's good of you to do this." The caseworker straightened the strands that had fallen and messed with the careful part in my dark hair. "He should fit right in, and I'm confident the others will like him. He's a quiet, thoughtful boy."

"We're happy to have him."

"You'll put him to work in the orchard?" she asked.

"Of course, there's always work for one more."

"Good. It's just a month," she insisted, "maybe two, and we'll have a permanent adoptive family for him."

"Understood."

The tall and thin but sturdy man's name was Mr. Wayne Bevan. He told me I could call him whatever I liked.

I called him Father.

He called me John. Never Bud, Champ, Pal, Tiger, Kiddo, or Cowboy. He said he called me John because John was my name. It was also the name of the EMT who delivered me, and no one had ever wanted to change it after they put it on my bassinet in the hospital's nursery.

A month passed and the caseworker with the heavy perfume and tennis shoes never called, at least not that I knew. I saw her come by once, after two months, to check on me and report on her office's progress. Just the two of us went for a walk around the orchard, and she asked me the same questions I'd been asked when staying in other homes.

I overheard their discussion at the kitchen table. "He seems happy, yes? Is he eating? You have a magical place here, Mr. Bevan. It's just heavenly. Let's try another few months, okay? And it would make me feel a great deal better, Wayne, if you'd try again to give up the cigarettes. I'm covering for you."

"Of course," Father answered, "anything for the boys. I'll do it."

Whenever the woman came to check on me she added a few more months and thanked Father for being one of the good guys. On one of her last visits she gave Father a fancy ballpoint pen with the words "I did it!" engraved on the side. She also gave him a hug and said loud enough for everyone to hear, "I knew you could quit."

Eventually she stopped coming at all and before a judge at the county courthouse I became John Bevan. Permanently adopted. Just like Scott and Tim. The son of the orchardist on Middle Road.

Father said we were *survivors*.

Survivor. Sure, life on the orchard was hard. But it wasn't the living that was hard, it was the work, and despite my background I never felt like a *survivor*. There were long, grueling days every September, yes, when I felt spent and more like the seasonal workers who picked alongside us than the son of the orchardist who slept in a safe, comfortable bed in the house on the hill. But my childhood wasn't a broken tale of being overworked or neglected. It was a fluid story of red apples, yellow apples, and big brothers.

The others the caseworker referred to were two older boys my father cared for on the orchard and also adopted. Just like me, Scott and Tim both called him *Father*. I learned they'd both come from dangerous homes in Richmond, Virginia. They'd also both spent time in the foster system before landing at the orchard about seven months apart.

I was the youngest by six years; maybe that's why I was protected so well, treated so kindly. They taught me the ways of the orchard, where the creek was too deep for swimming alone, and how to sleep standing up when the fall harvest took such a toll that we lost sense of whether the sun was rising or setting.

During my first year on The Apple Orchard, as my father called it, Scott and Tim let me walk with them to the bus stop at the end of our long dirt-and-gravel driveway. It was 242 downhill steps from the concrete porch to the first row of trees that ran parallel to Middle Road. Father made us stop at that first row of trees standing guard some thirty feet from the busy country road. It was just a two-lane road, but it saw a lot of traffic as a popular shortcut from Strasburg to the big city of Winchester.

My brothers and I noticed that after every rainstorm a fresh line appeared in the driveway, drawn deep in the gravel and about the width of the heel of a work boot. Tim and Scott said the line was magic, and I played along at first, but I was pretty sure it was man-made.

Some boys would have tempted fate and traffic by venturing into the forbidden space between that line and the road.

I never thought to cross it.

As we waited for the bus Tim taught Scott and me things he'd learned roaming the streets of Richmond. He knew how to defend himself and his friends. He knew how to go hungry for three days without complaining.

More than anything he liked to tell stories about Grandpa Bevan, who he'd known better than Scott, and who I'd never even met.

Tim taught me that Father didn't like to hunt.

Thankfully he didn't mind if we did, and when my brother got his first rifle it was Grandpa Bevan who taught him to load it, fire it, clean it, and keep it locked away from curious fingers. I heard Father wasn't happy the night Grandpa walked in the front door holding that brand-new rifle. But Grandpa was persuasive, and he and Tim spent the next day practicing on tin cans and milk jugs on the western edge of the orchard.

Practice led to hunting trips that Tim said convinced him he was born two hundred years too late. If he'd had his way, he and Grandpa Bevan would have beaten Lewis and Clark to the Pacific Ocean at the Columbia River.

How I envied all that Grandpa taught him.

Finally the bus rolled into view. But only when it came to a complete stop did my brothers race across the line and up the high steps to their dark green back-row seats.

Some boys would have been embarrassed by their younger brother waving obnoxiously as the driver pulled the door shut and rolled away.

My brothers waved back and pressed their noses against the glass until the bus disappeared over the hill.

When I thought there was no chance of the bus coming back because someone had forgotten their library book or math homework, which never happened, I counted the 242 steps slowly back up the hill and reminded myself that if it was

Monday, Wednesday, or Friday, at least I had the firehouse by the preschool in Woodstock.

Sometimes in the afternoon, if my chores were done before my brothers were home from school, I prepared a snack for them at the kitchen counter. I put peanuts or pretzel rods and mini-marshmallows in plastic bags and met them at the magic line at the bottom of the driveway. When I forgot my own snack they would smile, share, and chase me with the threat of a noogie. But I didn't mind. Sometimes I even forgot on purpose.

My brothers told me detailed tales of cafeteria skirmishes and we trudged like tired Civil War soldiers back up the hill to our split-level green house in the middle of the orchard. If one of them acted ornery I'd puncture a marshmallow with a pretzel and pretend it was a gun. I'd pursue them in and around the trees that lined the driveway, aiming and firing with a "Kapowpow! You're down, soldier!"

Back then bad moods didn't last long at the orchard.

When I was still five, Father let both my brothers skip school and come to Woodstock for my preschool graduation. The other boys and girls had moms, dads, even grandparents. I had two brothers and a father. None related by blood, all bound by love, all smiling like I'd just graduated at the top of my class from Harvard Law.

When I was seven my brothers taught me to

identify the types of apples we grew. I learned the mostly red apples were Red Delicious, Gala, and Braeburn. The greens were easier to remember: They were Granny Smith and tasted good with peanut butter. The yellows were Golden Delicious and my favorite, Ginger Gold.

I also learned how many apples made a bushel, how many bushels filled the wooden crates or bins, and how many apples we needed to survive each year.

When I was eight my oldest brother, Tim, a high school junior, took me hunting in Timberville. I wasn't allowed to hold a loaded gun yet—Father's orders—but I still felt old and smart and brave when he let me carry a backpack with water, venison jerky, apples, and extra ammo. During lunch we sat on a stump big enough for both of us.

Tim let me hold the rifle.

I remember how heavy it was in my hands.

I remember how scared his eyes looked when he realized he hadn't unloaded it yet.

I remember how he barked at me when I tried putting the scope to my eye and placed my eager finger on the trigger. "You're gonna kill someone, John!"

I remember that one year later during a senior trip to Ocean City, Maryland, Tim drowned.

I cried for days that became weeks. I cried until Father took me to the doctor and asked if there was anything he could do. If I hadn't been crying, I might have been embarrassed that Father asked the question in front of me.

The doctor put his hand on Father's shoulder. "Wayne, you might try asking him *why* he's crying."

He did, and in the truck driving home I answered, "Who will keep me safe when you're not here?"

Father pulled to the side of Route 11 and held me in his arms.

I sobbed until my stomach hurt.

"I'll be here, John. Scott will be here, too. And the orchard will always, *always* be here."

My throat was so sore and dry I was surprised Father heard me ask, "Can we take the long way home?"

"John, I will never say no to the long way."

I fell asleep on his lap.

Father buried Tim in a familiar clearing at the highest point on the orchard.

Scott and I dug a much smaller hole next to him and buried the long end of a white cross Father made from the wood of an apple bin.

Father painted it just before every harvest until his last.

Four
The Bevans

T HE story of Wayne Bevan was painted slowly. It came to me a careful brushstroke at a time. Not because the painter was lazy or indifferent, but because the canvas was so treasured. Protected.

Each new detail prompted me to love him and the orchard more than the day before.

I discovered that my adoptive father was not the *original* orchardist of Middle Road. That was *his* father, Grandpa Bevan, who sold nearly everything and mortgaged the rest so he could buy and clear the land. Grandpa was in his forties, Father was finishing high school in Winchester, and Grandma Bevan was devastated that he'd quit his job for a tract of useless land and a prayer of farming apples.

The men hadn't yet sold a single apple when Grandma said she needed to move to Harrisonburg to care for her ailing mother. "She needs me," she told Grandpa. "Maybe I need her, too. It's just a break. A break, that's all. I must have time to come to terms with all this. It's only fair. I'll come home as often as possible."

As often as possible, according to Father, meant

just four times the first year. His birthday, a weekend to pick up some of her winter clothes, Easter, and another weekend to hunt for sewing supplies she'd left behind.

Grandpa called Grandma every Sunday night and told her the orchard and her men needed her.

But Grandma's mother always needed her more. She claimed to suffer from osteoporosis, arthritis, skin cancer, ulcers, sleep problems, diabetes, and thyroid disease. Father said once after watching a special report about prostate cancer on *60 Minutes,* she turned to her daughter and said, "Honey, I'm afraid my prostate hurts, too."

She died the next year in a nursing home.

Grandpa and Father went to the funeral. But Grandma decided that Harrisonburg had become her home, and the men came back to the orchard alone.

Grandpa was convinced the orchard would be a good balm for the wounds he and my father shared. It was. And so were the cartons of cigarettes they smoked together.

They worked from dawn to dusk, and sometimes beyond, six days a week until the hilly, imperfect ground became an orchard. Father said they lit up in the cool mornings when the smoke mixed with the fog. They smoked walking to and from the barn. To and from the house. To and from the mailbox. They smoked in rocking chairs on the front porch until darkness hid the rows of trees.

Grandpa said the orchard was like a woman who would develop on her own time and couldn't be rushed, no matter how badly they needed her to grow up. While they waited, they sold the lumber they'd cleared to pay the bills. When it ran out, they sold vegetables from their garden at a roadside stand. Grandpa even ventured off the orchard for occasional side jobs painting or fencing.

The wait nearly killed them, but their sweat equity paid off deliciously, and from the moment my father tasted his first Red Delicious apple from a tree he'd personally nurtured to maturity, he said he knew he'd never leave the orchard. Never.

When Father was twenty-eight he fell in love with a checker at a Food Lion in Front Royal where he found the best prices on their favorite brand of cigarettes.

They each turned thirty the same month they were married at her family's church.

She smiled the first time Father asked how long they'd wait for children.

He asked again a season later.

The answer was the same. "I'm sorry, Wayne, I've just never wanted kids."

They each turned thirty-four the same month she became bored with both Father and the orchard and drove away. Mutual friends said she moved to New York and took a job answering phones for an editor at some important publishing company. "She's just too big for the Valley," one of her girlfriends told Father. "She needed to fly."

Neither Father nor Grandpa would ever fully understand how or why the orchard had repelled the women they loved. All either man had wanted was for the orchard to bear fruit, teach a lesson or two about life and work, and become a permanent part of the Bevan legacy.

I never met Grandpa Bevan. By the time I arrived on the orchard, he'd passed away of natural causes. "There's no great story, John. No big accident, no disease. It was just his time." Father said he became worried one night when Grandpa didn't come off the orchard after spending the afternoon spraying. He found him slumped over his tractor midway down a row of Goldens. *It was just his time.*

Father, Tim, and Scott buried him in a grassy clearing on the orchard. Father said that was the first time he'd ever seen Tim cry. He also said Tim cleaned Grandpa's rifle at the kitchen table almost every night for weeks after he died.

The night they found Grandpa, Father pulled my brothers next to him and said that one day they would bury him right next to their grandfather, the way it should be.

It must have broken my father's heart that Tim would take his place in the clearing first.

Five
First Harvest

🌿

I'D noticed them before, but I didn't really *see* the roadside crosses until my first harvest.

It was early August at The Apple Orchard and we were harvesting the first fruit of the year, Ginger Golds, though there wasn't much I could do as a five-year-old. I filled water coolers, made bologna and cheese sandwiches every day for lunches, and served as a runner when someone needed something out of reach.

My brothers were old enough to do almost everything the seasonal workers did, and I watched with envy as they stood among the branches and plucked apples. They dropped them in their shoulder bags. When the bags became too heavy they stepped to the ground and placed them in the nearest bin, taking great care not to bruise them.

One of my favorite jobs was to walk beneath the trees and collect the good apples that fell. Father said it was fine to eat them, which I did, but they never tasted very good while my brothers were still on ladders, drenched in sweat and thick Virginia humidity.

Sometimes Father asked us not to eat certain

apples. Often the problem was obvious, an odd blemish, a persistent pest. But occasionally he was faced with questions even a lifetime of experience and the experts at the extension office didn't have answers to. My brothers and I always knew when Father needed answers. He would quietly excuse himself from the house and walk alone in the evening down every single row of the orchard.

"Where are you going?" I asked the first time he left for one of his special walks.

"To listen," he said.

"To God?"

"And the orchard."

Father always came back with answers.

I remember that whether or not they knew it at the time, Father was always trying to teach the employees to listen, too. He thought it made them more productive. He also thought they'd accomplish more if they were legal, documented seasonal workers. Most came from Mexico, and Father always insisted they be properly documented. If they didn't already speak some English, he encouraged them to learn as long as they were on the payroll. Most spoke just a few words but still communicated perfectly using what Father called the universal language of apple farming.

One year we had a man from Jamaica. He was friendly and always smiling. I loved listening to his musical accent, but I don't think I understood him much better than the Spanish speakers.

Scott, Tim, and I loved watching how the workers treated Father with such respect. He said they were kind and respectful because that's how he treated them, like good friends who would have spent time together anyway, even if there wasn't work to do on a fifty-three-acre orchard.

During harvest, the workers lived in a huge house we shared with another orchard in Winchester. In all there must have been thirty men in that house; certainly there were more men than places to sit and rest or eat a meal. At night they slept in cramped, military-style beds and shared two small bathrooms.

Still, I liked it when Father let me ride with him to pick the men up in the morning. I liked hearing their music and laughter as we pulled up to the front door. And because my name was easy to say, they said it a lot with more energy than anyone else. *"Qué tal? Qué tal, Juan?"*

Father said the world would be more peaceful if everyone worked and loved as hard as those men.

He must have, but I don't remember Father sleeping much during the harvest. Each morning he prepared a breakfast, but only when it was on the table and ready to eat would he roll my brothers and me from bed. I was so tired those mornings during my first harvest that I often fell asleep next to a bowl of oatmeal or plate of eggs and toast. Father let me rest until breakfast was finished and the table was cleared, but he always woke me before leaving the house. He said that if I was going to be a Bevan I'd need to learn to work, and I couldn't work sleeping at the table.

I was only five, but I already knew I wanted to be a Bevan much more than I wanted to sleep in.

On the hottest days when Father saw me laboring to stay awake, he'd ask me to go inside and make sure the two window air-conditioning units were working. "Why don't you turn them on and stay inside for an hour, just to be sure they stay on, okay, John?"

"Yes, sir." I panted and slowly marched, head down, toward the house. When I thought I couldn't be seen, I darted to a neighboring row of trees and ran as fast as I could to the front door. Usually long before an hour had passed, but after enough time that my T-shirt had dried, I walked back to whatever row of trees Father was toiling in and gave him a thankful hug. Then I worked at his side until the dinner call.

As the temperatures cooled and harvest ended, most of the workers from our orchard and the many others in the Shenandoah Valley made their way to jobs elsewhere. But because Father had been having back problems, he asked his two most trusted men—José Miguel and Mateo—to stay a few days longer and help deliver some of the apples we sold direct to grocery stores.

33

Though they were strangers to me, Father said they'd been to the orchard for harvest three years in a row. Father appreciated how they were always the first to work and the last to leave.

The two men drove The Apple Orchard truck between Petersburg, West Virginia, on Route 55 and east on 66 to Gainesville, Virginia. They delivered apples at towns small and smaller along the way.

Father was sitting at the kitchen table with a calculator doing what he called his "Apple Math" one evening, waiting for José Miguel and Mateo to return. A sheriff's deputy knocked on the screen door.

"Come in," Father said.

"Wayne," the deputy said as he stepped through the door, "is your white box truck missing?"

"Well no, I should think not. Why?"

"There's been an accident on 55 up by McCauley. Your truck is in the woods. We thought it might have been stolen."

"Stolen? Why? Are the men alright?"

My brothers and I were pretending to play cards on the floor in the living room.

The deputy noticed. "Step outside, if you would." He opened the door for Father and they stood close on the front porch. The truth was that from that spot we could hear even better. We scooted across the floor and sat beneath the open front window.

"Well?" Father's voice had an uncommon edge.

"They're both dead, Mr. Bevan. Dead before anyone could get there."

We couldn't see, but it sounded like Father sat in one of the four rocking chairs on the concrete front porch. I wanted to cry, but five-year-olds don't cry in front of their big brothers.

"You knew them then?" the sheriff asked.

Father didn't reply right away, and when the sheriff began to ask again he interrupted him.

"Of course I did. They worked for me. Mateo and José Miguel. They were driving back from Moorefield."

"I see then."

"But why? Why would you think the truck was stolen? These were good men, my very best workers. They worked on the orchard."

"Now, Wayne, we just didn't know what to think."

"Obviously," Father said with an even sharper edge. "Take me there."

A moment later Father and the deputy sped down the driveway and peeled onto Middle Road.

An hour later they returned and Father reported to us that the driver had drifted asleep and into a concrete bridge abutment.

A week later Father paid to fly the bodies home to Mexico.

After church the next Sunday Father drove us to the crash site. There were still black skid marks that snaked left, right, left, and right again—right into the side of a concrete bridge. The four of us planted two plain white crosses made from apple bin wood at the side of the road.

That was the day I started noticing crosses everywhere.

Six

Emma Jane

𝕬

EMMA Jane Elkington was the most beautiful eleven-year-old I'd ever seen.

Sandy Hook Elementary School. Strasburg. Fifth grade. Emma Jane sat one desk in front of me and one row to the right. The angle was perfect to gaze at her sweet-as-Mike-and-Ikes profile without being detected. On the occasions she turned and caught me staring, I pretended to have buckteeth and chewed on the top of my pencil like a carrot.

This made her smile, and that made me smile, and that brought teasing from a boy named Stuart who sat in front of me and saw everything. But Stuart didn't scare me; he was only ten. Besides, my brother Scott said he was almost positive I could take him in a fistfight.

Emma Jane kept smiling at me all through middle school, and I kept smiling back. Even when I kissed Jennifer Parker during field day in the library, I wished it were Emma Jane. When I asked Emma Jane to the eighth-grade graduation dance, she reminded me she couldn't date until she was sixteen. So I took Katie Whatshername instead. Katie was very pretty, too, and very blond, but she didn't smile at me like Emma Jane did.

During our first year at Strasburg High School, Emma Jane and I settled into very different camps. We still spoke, and I often rerouted myself through the halls to pass her between classes. But we had different friends. Different classes. Different clubs. Different goals.

Emma Jane was an honor roll student.

I was not.

Emma Jane wanted to be a teacher.

I wanted to grow apples.

Emma Jane was an energetic member of the Christian group Young Life.

I was not.

Emma Jane was very popular.

I was popular the week I climbed the goalpost and hung James Marshall's jockstrap like a flag. But the popularity faded faster than the black eye James gave me on the bus the next day.

I went with a few girls here and there, mostly because I hoped Emma Jane noticed. I never knew for sure if she did, but she still had a smile that I swore was reserved for me and me alone.

Near the end of our sophomore year, between first and second period, on her sixteenth birthday, I slipped a note in Emma Jane's locker asking her to come with me to the drive-in in Stephens City on Saturday night.

During lunch she returned the favor. *Yes to a date. No to the drive-in!* She used a tiny smiley face as the point of her exclamation.

I replied immediately on the back of the same piece of paper. *Roller-skating at Stoney Creek?*

The note was back in my locker again by the time the dismissal bell freed us for the weekend. *Perfect! Call me!*

I called that night to arrange the time and offered to pick her up in my father's new quad-cab truck.

"I can't ride with you alone, or any boys yet," she said on the phone, "but the truck sounds lots of fun. Maybe your dad could drive us?"

I'd waited five years for a date with Emma Jane and now my father was going to be our chap-erone? "No problem, I'll ask." I found him sitting in a rocker on the front porch, and he agreed with an old-man wink. I went back to the phone. "He says okay. Pick you up at seven-thirty?"

"I need to be home by nine, John."

Nine? I'd been on dates starting that late. "Alright, how about six-thirty?"

"Perfect for me. I can't wait!"

The way she said it, so pure, so innocent, it

made the dark hairs on my arms shoot straight into the air.

Two nights later I showed up at her door in new Levi's that were so stiff I could barely get out of the truck. I'd also bought a new dress shirt that afternoon, a navy blue button-down collar from JCPenney in Winchester. I wore four dabs of cologne I'd sampled at the mall and a pair of tennis shoes that I'd spent an hour scrubbing dirt from.

I expected Emma Jane's dad to meet me at the door with a shotgun and his cleaning cloth—I'd seen it before—but when he opened the door, he simply extended his hand.

"Hi, John," he said, and we shook hands. We'd met before but I'd never noticed how smooth his hands were. He didn't have the calluses my own father had.

"Good evening, Mr. Elkington."

"Emma Jane will be right down."

"Thank you, sir."

"You know this is her first date, yes?"

I nodded.

"She's been waiting a long time for this night."

So have I, I thought.

"You'll treat her like a lady?" he asked, looking down at me through his reading glasses. "Tonight and every day and night after?"

"Of course. My father taught me right."

He looked from me out to our truck parked on

the street. He shot him a two-fingered wave that could have been mistaken for a peace sign.

Father nodded back.

"Your father is a good man," Mr. Elkington said.

"I know—"

If either of us said anything else during the next thirty seconds, I sure don't remember it. I only remember how beautiful Emma Jane looked with her hair brushed and held together on top with a red clip. Her shirt was red, too, and her jeans were also Levi's, but not nearly as tight as most of the girls wore them. Or even as tight as mine.

"John." Mr. Elkington turned to me. "Would you mind waiting with your dad in the truck a moment? She'll be right there."

I was probably *in* the truck before he'd even finished the request.

I rolled my window halfway down, and Father and I watched the scene unfold like a drive-in movie with bad speakers outside the car windows that only gave sound every few words or phrases.

Mr. Elkington hugged his daughter for the longest time. It looked like he was whispering something, but from my distance I'd never know what. He released her but kept his hands on her arms. He looked at me, then back at Emma Jane, said something with a serious look of fatherly concern, and she covered her mouth in surprise.

"Heavens no!" I think she said.

I heard Father snicker next to me in the truck. "What?"

"Nothing, son. Nothing at all." He cleared his throat, and we both kept our eyes fixed on the front porch drama.

Emma Jane burst into laughter then bounced into the house. A moment later she reappeared on the porch, flung her arms around her dad's neck, kissed him on the cheek, mumbled something else I couldn't quite make out, then yelled good-bye and scampered down the walk toward the truck. "See you by nine o'clock! I love you!" Finally words we didn't have to guess at.

As she approached me I thought she beamed brighter than the headlights on a semi. Radiant. Brilliant. I gave her a cheesy grin and waved back.

Father nudged me, and I got out of the front seat and left the door open. I helped her in, even though she didn't really need it, and got into the back.

As we drove down 81 toward Edinburg I listened to Emma Jane and my father make small talk up front. He told a few jokes, each more funny than the last, and Emma Jane giggled and told a few of her own. They sounded not like an old man and his son's young date, but old friends with mature souls and pure hearts.

I spoke hardly a word. I was comfortable sitting in the back and wondering why Emma Jane made me feel something no other girl ever had.

Later that evening we skated in a wide, slow circle around the rink under low lights and a spinning disco ball.

Faith Hill sang "Breathe."

Emma Jane reached over and took my hand in hers.

I didn't say it, but I knew then that I loved her. And I knew I always would.

I prayed she'd love me and the orchard, too. And I prayed the orchard would love her back.

Seven

The Fence

IT could have been worse; I could have killed him.

Teddy and Emma Jane had AP Geometry together, and I knew he'd made some third-rate passes at her before. But Emma Jane fended him off with a polite smile and refresher that she was dating me. Exclusively.

Emma Jane insisted she didn't know what had triggered Teddy's heightened efforts to win some affection, but they culminated with a suggestive drawing Teddy slipped in her geometry textbook with the headline: *I'd like to practice these angles with you.*

I'd been in a few fights before and I was comfortable with the power of adrenaline. But when Emma Jane showed me the drawing in the parking lot after school, the moment sent me to a place that scared both of us.

"Please don't do anything silly, John. He's just a dumb boy."

"Exactly. A dummy who needs a lesson."

"No, John. Graduation is a month away. Don't ruin it for us. Let it go, please? I'll switch desks and pretend it never happened. Alright?"

As she spoke I shredded the drawing into tiny pieces of confetti.

"John?"

"Yeah."

"You won't fight him?"

"Not if you don't want me to."

She leaned in and kissed me. "I don't, but I love that you would."

I drove her home and raced to the orchard. Father was at the university extension getting advice on a pest that was testing his patience and resisting the sprays.

My brother Scott was gone, too. But he hadn't lived at home in six years. He was finishing a law degree at George Mason, class of 2001.

At the back edge of the orchard we had a small storage barn for whatever apples we didn't sell immediately after the harvest. Some went direct to grocers, some went to an applesauce plant, and the most imperfect apples went to juice for a fraction of their real worth. But some bad apples didn't leave the storage barn until Father or I cleaned them out, and sometimes that didn't happen as quickly as it should have.

I parked my truck by the house and drove a four-wheeler through the orchard and back to the barn. There they were, rotting away nicely in two bins in the corner. We'd discovered them long after the harvest, hiding among a high stack of empty bins, and Father had asked me to dispose of them weeks ago.

I took one of the bins—three, maybe four bushels—and heaved it up and onto the back of the four-wheeler. Then I drove back to my truck, one hand on the wheel, one on the bin, and loaded the bin in the truck bed. I drove south to Teddy's house on Back Road in Toms Brook.

Teddy wasn't there, but his white 1989 Mustang big block was. And lucky for both of us, I didn't have to break any windows.

I opened the driver's-side door and dumped the wet, rotting apples onto his front seats. When the seats couldn't hold any more, the apples spilled onto the floorboards and the smell exploded up and filled the car. It was darkly sweet, fermented, like the final breath of a homeless alcoholic.

I considered leaving a note. A marker. Some sign to be sure Casanova Teddy knew who'd stopped by for a visit. But 120 rotten apples were probably enough.

Later that night I sat at my father's computer, the only one in the house, struggling to finish an eight-page paper on the Battle of Cedar Creek. I heard a car roll up the driveway and didn't need to look outside to know who it was.

I caught fragments through the open window as Teddy and his dad greeted Father by the maple tree. "Rotten apples . . . Teddy . . . Mustang . . . Leather . . . Teddy . . . Emma Jane . . . John . . . Boundaries . . . Sorry . . . Again . . . Please . . ."

The exchange couldn't have lasted more than three minutes, and Teddy and his father vanished before I had a chance to prepare a defense. Father called me outside.

"John."

"Yes, sir."

"This true?"

"Yes, sir."

"This really about Emma Jane?"

I nodded.

"Is she in trouble?"

"Not anymore."

Father looked out at the orchard. "Good. Now do you need me to tell you—"

"No, sir."

His eyes moved from the rows of trees to the house and back. "Tomorrow after school. Straight home. No Emma Jane. No pool in Front Royal."

"Alright."

"I have a project for you."

Just before bed Scott called from his apartment in Arlington. He thought the episode was much funnier than Father had.

After school the next day I returned home to stacks of wood, a posthole digger, nails, and five gallons of white paint. Father had stuck short orange construction flags in the ground every ten feet or so in a huge rectangle that encompassed the tree, the cross marking Tim's grave, most of the grass surrounding the house, and, of course, the house itself.

I surveyed the punishment.

Father appeared from behind the house. "It's for a fence."

I did not say what first crossed my mind. "Okay," I said instead.

"You're going to build yourself a fence."

"Build *myself* a fence or build it *by* myself?"

"Both."

I dropped my backpack on the ground. "Why?"

"Because I've always thought we needed one, John. A white picket fence. It is protection. It marks the land as ours. The pickers don't always understand that the orchard is theirs to freely roam, but the grass around this house is our own. It is private. The fence will be a reminder to all of us that this isn't just an orchard, John, it is a home." Father put his hand on my shoulder. "And your wife, whomever that will be, just might want a white picket fence like all the commercials show . . . Moreover, it will be good for you."

Though I'd tested the boundaries during my teens, especially since Scott had graduated and moved on to college, I still respected my father too much to argue. I wanted to protest, earnestly in fact, but I couldn't. Plus, I knew all it would accomplish is growing the project so large I'd soon be encompassing the entire Shenandoah Valley in a fence you could see from space.

"Will you be helping me?"

"I did," Father said, pointing to the supplies and then to the orange flags marking the future fence line. Then he let slip a rare smile that said, *You'll thank me for this later.*

I smiled back and shook my head.

I wasn't smiling the next night, or the night after that, or on most of the nights after spending the day at school, doing homework, my regular orchard chores, and then wrapping up the day by digging holes and building the fence.

Scott came home one weekend and offered to help, but Father wouldn't allow it. "It's his fence, son, John should build it."

But a few days later Father made a surprising concession. "Emma Jane. She can help."

"Really?"

"If she'd like."

She did, and finishing the fence with her at my

side in the evenings made it seem more like a reward than a punishment for a crime I hardly remembered anymore. Especially since the wind picked up the smell of her hair, mixed it with the pleasant pureness of outdoor paint and apple blossoms, and ran it right by my nose. I took that smell to bed with me every night.

When we were nearly done, Father helped install the two gates, one in the front by the maple tree and one in the back by the shed. We finished painting on the same June weekend we graduated from Strasburg High School. Emma Jane wanted to paint the final stroke together and put her hand on top of the brush, just above mine, and we covered the final naked spots of brown with bright white.

With paint still on the brush, Emma Jane ripped it from my hand and swiped it across my face, coating my nose and the tops of both cheeks under my eyes. I tackled her on the soft grass and sat on top of her. "Do you know what you've started?"

She was laughing too hard to answer, covering her face and kicking her legs under me.

I pried the brush from her hand and painted her nose. Then I rubbed my nose against hers.

Emma Jane giggled and I kissed her. Then again. And again. Each kiss deeper and more intense than the last.

She rolled over and out from underneath me.

"That's enough, Tom Sawyer. You know I've made a promise." Emma Jane sat cross-legged and pulled blades of grass from her hair.

I flopped down on my back and groaned as dramatically as I could.

"Oh hush up. I'm *still* waiting. *I* know it. *You* know it. *God* knows it." She bent down and kissed me on the forehead. Then she lay back on the grass at my side, taking my hand and interlocking her fingers with mine. "John Bevan. The fence is beautiful, it really is."

"Beautiful? It's a fence."

"Maybe to you. But to your dad it's more than that. You should be proud of this."

"I suppose so."

She started to say something but instead replaced the words with a kiss on my nose.

"I really love your dad," she said, pulling away.

"Huh?"

"I do. He's a good man."

"Where in the world did *that* come from?"

"Just thinking how lucky I am. You're going to be just like him."

"Smart?" I fired. "Handsome?"

"Just smart," she wrinkled her nose. "Seriously, he's more than smart. He's *wise*."

"I suppose so."

She sighed. "My dad is great, too. I mean, you know how much I love my dad." She sighed again, and I wasn't sure if she was just sighing or searching for words. "I'm just grateful we both have strong dads that love us. Not all kids get that. And I've learned *so much* from mine." She looked at me. "You know what? If anything ever happened to my dad, I know yours would be there to lead me through whatever came along."

"Of course he would. I'd be there, too."

She looked back to the sky. "Can you believe we're actually high school graduates?"

"I can believe *you're* a high school graduate, I just can't believe *I* am."

She laughed. "Good point."

We stared up at the high clouds and stayed quiet. Not because we had nothing to say, but because it was comfortable. Off in the distance I heard my father's tractor moving from one row to another, spraying for pests.

"I bet your mother would be proud of you," Emma Jane said, staring into the sky.

"You think?"

"Well *of course* she would be."

"I hope you're right."

There was nothing Emma Jane Elkington didn't know about me. I'd told her about my arrival on the orchard, Tim's accident, Grandpa Bevan, my mother. I'd even shown her the manila folder with the police reports from the night we passed each other at the edge of life.

She gave my hand a squeeze. "Do you miss her?"

"Hard to miss someone you didn't know." But I knew that's not what she meant. "Yeah, I miss having a mother, for sure." I watched a plane streak across the sky, leaving behind a white line between two odd-shaped clouds.

"Do you ever wonder what she was like?"

I had. Often. "Sometimes, I guess so. I think she was pretty and smart but not book smart like you, more street smart like me. I bet she had to be. She was probably weak though, too. Afraid. Why else would she run? I don't know."

I looked to Emma Jane and saw the same thoughtful expression she gave when she prayed over meals or at church. Only at that moment her lips weren't moving.

"But it doesn't matter. And I don't really know anything more than the reports tell me. She danced. Must have loved it."

"Yes." Emma Jane picked up the thought. "And when she danced she felt free, no worries in the world. I wish you could have seen her dance just once. She must've looked beautiful in her dancing outfits."

"I like that."

"Let's remember her that way until we ask her ourselves."

It was another of a million moments that I reminded myself how lucky I was to have Emma Jane at my side.

"You know, Emma Jane"—I was surprised to

feel even more coming—"I'm not lying, a mom would have been good. But the orchard has been great, too, almost like a mother, that's what my father says. And like you said, he's been the best. I don't ever think about him not being my *real* father, you know what I mean?"

She grinned.

"Now I'm just jabbering, sorry."

"Don't you dare." She flicked my ear. "What about your *other* father? The older man your mother loved. Do you think about him?"

"I used to when I was a kid. But if he didn't want to know about me, then why would I want to know about him now? He might as well be dead."

Emma Jane glanced at me in obvious disapproval.

"You know what I mean, he's just some guy in the city who took advantage of my lonely mother."

She looked heavenward. "Have you ever been to your mom's grave?"

"Just once. My father took me a few weeks after I turned sixteen. She's buried up in Fairfax. Nothing fancy. Just a metal marker with her name on it."

"Take me sometime?"

"Really?"

"Uh-huh." She scanned the sky. "See that cloud?" Emma Jane pointed with her free hand. "What does that look like?"

"A squirrel."

"A squirrel?" She cackled. "Wrong. Bzzzzz. Try again."

"Hmm, our school mascot. A ram."

"You're terrible at this," she said. "Look closer, it's Lord Fairfax Community College."

I squinted my eyes. "Oh yeah, I see it now. Clear as day. Bet you never thought it would get here." I looked south in the sky. "See that one?"

"Which?"

"There," I guided her index finger. "That one. The superhandsome one. That's me smiling. Happy you're not going any farther away to school than Middletown."

"Right. And that angry-looking gray cloud right behind that one? See it? That's my dad wishing I'd gone to school out-of-state, *faaaaar* away, and studied accounting." She tried to say it without laughing, but me tickling her ribs didn't help.

"My turn," I said, pointing down the skyline over my feet. "See those two clouds stuck together?"

"Uh-huh."

"That's me and you."

Emma Jane took my hand again.

"But that's not me and you *today*. That's me and you in a year. Then five years. Then twenty years. Then a hundred years."

"No kids, Mr. Weatherman?"

"Well sure. Watch those two big clouds long

53

enough and a small cloud will show up. Maybe even two. I promise."

We dreamt away the rest of the afternoon, naming clouds and making predictions. Life with Emma Jane, even though she'd been on the fringes of my orchard for much of the time since our eleven-year-old introduction, had never been as sweet as that afternoon.

A finished fence.

A kept promise.

Kisses more red and more sweet than a Red Delicious apple.

Three months later on Labor Day I knelt on the banks of the Shenandoah River and, with her father's reluctant blessing, proposed. I slipped a simple ring with a tiny diamond on her finger. For a month I'd been rehearsing something more eloquent, but in the moment all that came out was, "Marry me?"

"Yes!"

We kissed and I lifted her off the ground, swinging her around in a circle just the way I'd imagined. "You've made me the happiest guy in the Valley, Emma Jane."

We twirled again. "Just the Valley?" she said as I put her down. "Not all of Virginia?"

I'd controlled my raging boyhood urges for three years with Emma Jane, but I thought once it was official, even with a long engagement, it would be easier.

It wasn't.

I kissed her ear as we kicked our feet in the river water.

"We've waited so long, John, what's a bit more? I promised Mom and Dad I'd be *at least* nineteen before I ever got married, and I think it's smart. What's another year?"

Another year was twelve more months of imagining my first night with Emma Jane as my wife, not a girlfriend with a curfew.

One summer night after a day together at the National Zoo in Washington, D.C., I returned home to the orchard and found Father still awake in the living room doing his Apple Math. He read me nearly as well as Emma Jane did.

"Fun night?"

"I guess."

Father looked up from his notebook and calculator. "It's difficult, isn't it?"

"What?"

"Waiting."

How does he know so much? I thought. "Yeah. You could say that."

"You're doing the right thing, John."

"I guess."

"Don't just guess, John, you are. You are honoring her."

"It's just getting more frustrating, not less. I just want to be married, move in, start our life. I've been waiting forever."

"Forever, John?"

"You know what I mean. Since sixteen. That's a long time. 'Cause I've always known it would be her in the end."

Father smiled again. I wondered if it was a side effect of growing old; his emotions were more obvious than they'd ever been.

"You'll be together a long time, John. A long, long time. What's another few dates that end in a little physical frustration if it makes you stronger? Makes her stronger, too."

"I guess."

Father took his glasses off, folded them up, and stuck them in his shirt pocket. "You ever been to Kansas, John?"

"Come on, you know I haven't."

"Oklahoma?"

"Father—"

"No then. Let me tell you what Midwest farming is like . . . It's flat . . . The property lines and crop rows are long and straight, like they were cut by God's table saw. You can stand at the end of your farm and not see past a row or two. It's flatter than flat. Corn, grains, whatever it is, it's hard farming and an equally hard life, but it's a more perfect farming."

"And."

"Apple farming isn't."

"Perfect?"

"No. None of it, John. Apple farming is hilly,

the rows haphazard, the ground knobby and imperfect. The orchard needs pruning, needs to be kneaded, thinned, massaged every day for a good crop. And don't you love how from Tim and Grandpa Bevan's graves on the high point you can see the entire orchard? All fifty-three rolling, messy, root-ridden, beautiful acres."

I was both listening intently and wondering if I'd ever be as wise or as good a father.

Father stood up. "Follow me. I have an idea." He led me to the shed behind the house, pulled the chain light, and picked up a gallon of paint and a brush. "Come."

I followed him out of the shed and to the picket fence along the back of the house.

Then he handed me the paint and brush. "Some people take cold showers. Some sing hymns. You'll paint."

"Huh?"

"You'll paint. Every time you feel . . . frustrated . . . you come out here and touch up the fence. It will take your mind off things."

He was right. I painted by moonlight for an hour that night. And by the time Emma Jane and I were married at the Valley Baptist Church in Edinburg, the fence was so white it belonged in heaven.

Eight
Good-bye, Honeycrisp

EMMA Jane and I were married on Sunday, September 1, 2002.

Scott was my best man. He wore a tuxedo he'd bought and the shiniest dress shoes I've ever seen.

Father wore a rented tuxedo and cowboy boots.

Scott brought his girlfriend, April, a law clerk at the firm he'd joined in McLean. She had a fun personality and might have been the prettiest girl at the wedding if it weren't for my new wife.

Emma Jane wore her mother's modest white wedding dress with a short train. Her hair was up, which wasn't my favorite, but it had a Cinderella quality that made it impossible for me to look away from her, even during the longer-than-expected service and reception after.

Emma Jane's parents had insisted on paying for everything, even though Father assured them last year's harvest had been good and he could contribute. The dinner was nice, much nicer than we needed. The music was from a live band and not from my friend Chris, the DJ in Woodstock with more CDs than anyone I knew. The photographer was a professional from Chantilly, even though

Father had purchased a new digital camera from Walmart just for the occasion.

It was all as her parents planned and as Emma Jane had sketched in her journal years earlier. It was precisely what she wanted. So, as Father taught me, that meant I wanted it, too. And I did.

We spent our wedding night at the Inn at Narrow Passage in Woodstock. Emma Jane's promise was worth waiting for. Three times, in fact, before we drove to the airport and spent four more days in Florida, another gift from her parents.

We returned and moved into a rented shabby townhouse in Stephens City. When I carried Emma Jane across the threshold, she accidentally kicked the door and the hinge on top pulled right from the doorjamb. But when we were inside and the shades were down and the door was locked, it felt like a palace.

The townhouse was located near the interstate, not far from the orchard and not far from campus where Emma Jane's classes began two days after we moved in. Every morning she went to class or the library to study, dreaming of being an elementary school teacher, while I went to the orchard to help with the harvest. In the evening, we rushed home to be together.

Sometimes we were careful. Sometimes we weren't.

"Lou Lou" Bevan was born a month after our

first anniversary. She looked so much like her mother I asked if Emma Jane had special ordered her that way. The eyes, the chin, the nose and tiny crease on the bridge, they were all borrowed from her genetically blessed mother.

Most important, our angel was born in the safety of a hospital and not on the side of the road in a winter storm. She was perfect.

When Lou Lou was just eight weeks old, Father called all of us to Sunday dinner at the orchard. First he asked if Scott and I remembered how much he'd smoked when we were kids on the orchard. Then he reminded us it was a nasty habit that he'd be very disappointed if any of his boys, or their children, or their children's children ever adopted. Then he admitted to having seen a doctor the week before. And finally, he said what we all feared. "I have lung cancer. It's bad and it will take me."

"How is that possible?" Scott asked.

"How far along is it?" Emma Jane wanted to know.

I just looked at him and said, "Thank you for being my father when you didn't have to be."

No one cried that evening more than Emma Jane. Hours later, sitting in the truck in front of our townhouse, she didn't even bother wiping the tears as she told me one of the few stories I'd never heard about my father.

We both knew when Emma Jane began

researching colleges during our senior year that it was mostly to appease her parents. Her dad, especially, had long expected Emma Jane to become an accountant or financial advisor and take over the successful family firm. But they'd never asked her. If they had, they would have known Emma Jane's dreams were in the classroom.

Between sobs and hiccups, Emma Jane told me that a meeting between our fathers changed the course of her life. My father, the unassuming, traditional, private, and nonconfrontational Wayne Bevan, visited Emma Jane's parents and skillfully made the case that by discouraging her dreams of being a teacher, they were stealing from her and every student who would ever sit and stare up at her, willing to move a mountain if she'd ask. He'd convinced Bob and Michelle that because they'd taught her so much and so well, she was now destined to be a teacher forever.

I never read it, but that same night while I sat on the couch and imagined life without my father, Emma Jane sat in the kitchen and wrote him an eight-page letter. In it she included a picture of the two of them at our high school graduation. Dad was smiling. Emma Jane was holding a wax apple he'd given her to place on her desk in her first classroom as a teacher.

In the last picture we ever took of him, Father is holding Lou Lou and smiling just as big. She was ten months old and sitting on his lap in a rocker on the front porch at the orchard. In the photo's background I see the fence and trunk of the towering maple. Lou Lou's cheeks were round and full, her thin dark hair gathered into a bow on top, like the stem of a perfect apple.

Father called her his little Honeycrisp.

We buried him in a clearing at the highest point on the orchard next to Grandpa Bevan and Tim. We planted another white cross, made from the wood of an apple bin, and painted it with leftover fence paint I found in the shed.

That night after family and friends had cleared off the orchard, I walked the rows alone and wondered if I'd learned everything I needed to know to become the orchardist, and not just the son. One after another, kicking through the tall grass that had gone to seed and watching puffs of pollen gather and break into tiny pieces.

I missed Father that night, but knowing Emma Jane was waiting for me on the front porch kept the tears from getting any further than my mind. I thanked God, literally and out loud, that she was there for me to soften the fall.

The next day in an attorney's office by the courthouse in Woodstock, the fifty-three-acre orchard and its twenty-two thousand trees were given equally to Scott and me. But Scott said as long as I wanted to live on it and run it the best way I knew how, it was all mine. "He wanted this.

And I love you, John. I'll do whatever I can for you. But the orchard has never been my dream."

"I know."

"But you've been preparing for this since the day you showed up. Haven't you?"

"I think so. Maybe I've always known this was going to be my life."

Over dinner that night I proposed anew to Emma Jane. "Emma Jane Bevan, I know you didn't ask for this. It's too much and too soon. And I know it's going to be hard . . . But I need you."

"Of course." She slid her plate and water glass to the side and exposed her palms.

I placed mine against hers. "Emma Jane, will you apple farm with me?"

"I will."

"It's a hard life, Emma Jane, and I cannot explain it, but it's been too much for other women before you."

She squeezed my hands. "If you're there, and I'm there, then it's where I want to be."

We broke our lease in Stephens City and moved onto the orchard immediately. She continued taking classes, part-time, with a dream of one day teaching at the same elementary school where we met.

Emma Jane liked it all: the orchard, the fruit, the life of the orchardist's wife. But I think she loved her fence most.

"Look closely," she told us one Sunday afternoon while sharing a picnic with Lou Lou on the
grass by the maple tree. "It's not just a fence, it's
a series of crosses, linked side by side, just like
you and me."

Nine

Fair

꽃

LOU Lou loved two things most: animals and
cotton candy.

That made the Shenandoah County Fair at the
Fairgrounds in Woodstock her own street in
heaven the last week of every August.

When she was two we went twice and she left
screaming both times.

When she was three we went three times on the
promise of no screaming.

When she was four we went four times and she
had her first chili dog. She threw it up on the
Zipper, which meant she threw it up on several
other people, too.

When she was five we gave her a clear set of
rules en route on the fair's opening Saturday.

"Lou Lou," Emma Jane said, turning around in
the minivan and looking right at her wide-eyed
daughter, "you stay close to Mommy and Daddy,
alright? No running off."

"Yes, ma'am."

"And only one cotton candy today, alright? And only after some lunch."

"Chili dogs?" she squeaked.

I nearly swore; fortunately I laughed instead.

"Not this year, Lou, maybe chicken?"

We rode the rest of the way south listening to Lou Lou make a list of everything she was going to see.

"First the cows. Then the pigs. Baby pigs, too. And the chickens and the baby chickens. Roosters. I like the roosters. Did they have bunnies last year? I remember a fat one. Oh oh oh, and then the lambs and the baby lambs. Or if we don't have time, just their babies. They are so cute, Mommy."

We exited 81 in Woodstock and sat in a long line of traffic making its way to Ox Road and the fairground entrance. The rides were already lit and spinning and twirling in the distance.

"And rides! First the Ferris wheel. And the swings. They better have swings again. Think I'll be tall enough for the bumper cars this year? And the slide! Remember the slide, Mommy? I'm so good on the slide. I'm fast."

"Not as fast as *I* am," I said.

"Uh-huh! Am, too! You're just a silly sack of apples, Daddy!"

We pulled in and were directed by volunteers in orange vests to the next open spot in the grass parking lot. Emma Jane slowly eased out of the van and opened Lou Lou's door. "Remember, Lou, Mommy can't ride with you this year? Not with baby Willard still in my tummy. But Daddy will ride *whatever* you want. Right, Daddy?"

"You get all the breaks," I said, and her eyebrows lifted and creased her tired forehead. Then her eyes repeated what they'd been saying for the entire thirty-eight weeks of her pregnancy. *Want to trade places?*

I took Lou Lou's hand with my right and Emma Jane's with my left. I squeezed both their hands three times. *I love you.*

They both squeezed back four times. *I love you, too.*

We explored every tent, every barn, every display, and petted every animal she could reach. I held her up to the ones she couldn't.

Emma Jane tried to follow us as Lou Lou admired every living creature in every single stall, but the thick, soupy smells of manure and fur sent her fast-walking for cleaner air.

Later, while we stood in the line for the slide, Lou Lou asked, "Did Grandpa like the fair just like me?"

"He sure did, darling. He brought me and Uncle Scott every year."

"Did he like the slide?"

"Sure."

"Did he slide in the burlap sack or on his behind?"

"I think he liked the sack. It made him go faster." I'd never seen him actually take the slide, but if he had, I'm sure he would have liked it.

"Was he fast like me?"

"Faster!"

"Uh-uh! No way!"

"Well then, *almost* faster."

A woman took our tickets, handed us two scratchy burlap sacks, and we hiked up the narrow, slowly rising stairs. From the top, before we sat in our lanes, we could see Emma Jane sitting at a picnic table below eating a strawberry funnel cake drowning in whipped cream. The glow of pregnancy was visible even from the top of the Tidal Wave Slide. I yelled to her, and Lou Lou and I each blew a kiss. She caught them, smooshed them together in her hands, and sprinkled them on top of her funnel cake before taking an exaggerated big bite.

Lou Lou and I sat on our burlap sleds and flew down the baby blue slide, over the three humps, pushing ourselves along for extra speed. After the final hill, I dug both my tennis shoes into the sides of my lane enough to slow myself and ensure she beat me to the soft mats at the bottom.

We repeated this twice more. Once because I wanted a rematch, and once just because she asked.

We ate Shaffer's barbeque chicken and baked

beans under a shelter with friends we knew from Central High.

After dinner we listened as the demolition derby drivers started their engines.

For dessert I had two scoops of homemade ice cream and a large fresh-squeezed lemonade.

Lou Lou had cotton candy.

Emma Jane had a little of everything.

The sun drifted down to the horizon, and Emma Jane's feet and back began to hurt. An unhappy Lou Lou was coaxed into leaving with one turn tossing Ping-Pong balls into empty goldfish bowls and two turns squirting high-pressure water into a bull's-eye to send a plastic monkey up a tree faster than anyone else. With my help steadying her hands, she won a pink bunny and left the fair with a smile on her face.

"Daddy, can we take the long way?"

"Lou Lou, I think Mommy needs to get home. She's pretty tired. I bet brother is tired, too."

"It's okay, John, I don't mind. As long as I'm off my feet. We can take the long way for Lou Lou."

I turned left on Route 42 away from the interstate and left again, northbound on Route 11. The two-lane highway ran parallel to 81 and was much slower, but still delivered us all the way to Strasburg, just a few miles from the orchard.

We passed through Woodstock, then Maurertown and Toms Brook. Emma Jane rested her head against the window and looked peacefully out at the fields disappearing in the gray-black evening air.

I looked at Lou Lou in the rearview mirror, fighting sleep, snuggling her pink bunny, a spot of cotton candy stuck to the corner of her mouth. I wished my father were there to appreciate how beautiful his little Honeycrisp had become.

I looked back to the front.

I think he came from my left.

Thaboom! The deer's impact was harder and the sound more violent than I thought possible. His body somersaulted in the air and landed on the right shoulder.

I slammed the brakes, fishtailing the van and settling on the shoulder. Two wheels on pavement, two on grass.

"Daddy! Daddy!"

"It's alright, Lou, we're alright."

Emma Jane sat up and placed both hands on her belly.

"Are you okay?" I put my hand on her belly, too. "Everything okay?"

"Just startled, that's all. I didn't see him, did you?"

"Not until I hit him."

I turned around to check on Lou Lou. She was turned backward, leaning over the backseat looking through the glass. "Is he okay, Daddy?"

"I don't know, darling, probably not, but it's for—"

"He's up! He's up!" she chirped and the deer rose and staggered off the side of the road into the clearing next to us. "He's alright!"

But before I could speak the deer stumbled and fell into a heap.

"Daddy!"

Once again I hesitated a moment too long. Lou Lou opened the van's automatic door, forced herself through a tiny sliver of space, and ran toward the injured animal.

"Lou! Stop!" I yelled and threw open my own door. A truck's horn wailed at me and it whizzed by so close it felt like my shirt could have blown off. I passed in front of the van and put my hand up to Emma Jane. *Stay here,* I mouthed. As I rounded the corner of the van I stepped through shards of broken headlamps and noticed blood and deer fur on the smashed grill.

By the time I arrived at the grassy clearing, Lou Lou was kneeling beside the deer and whispering near its bloodied head. "Wake up. Please wake up."

I knelt next to her. "It's alright, Lou Lou."

Her voice quivered, and if it hadn't been so dark, I was certain I'd see tears flowing freely down both her dirty cheeks. "I think he's dying, Daddy."

"I know, darling. I know."

She took my hand and leaned her head into my arm. "Can we say a prayer? For his mommy?"

There are sounds and words we do not forget.
A child praying.
A baby's first cries in a hospital delivery room.
That same child's first words.
The voice of a woman saying *I do* in her mother's white wedding dress. Not white because of fashion, white because she earned it.
The sound your very first car makes the very first time you turn the key.
The sound a truck makes when it brakes hard. Loses control. Crashes at fifty-miles-per-hour into a minivan parked on the side of a two-lane country road. Falls on its side.
I stood and turned.
I probably screamed for help as I ran toward the van, now resting well off the road and facing the opposite direction.
The airbags were deployed.
I heard Emma Jane crying. "The baby! John! The baby! My baby!"
Someone I did not know called for help.
Someone else I did not know gathered a panicky Lou Lou in his arms.
Two shiny engines arrived from the firehouse on Court Street in Woodstock. Paramedics in an ambulance also arrived and pulled Emma Jane out of the van and to the ground. Dark red blood rushed from her. On the roadside under flashing lights they delivered the body of our baby boy.
But he was not in it.

I rode with Emma Jane to the hospital and held her hand. Two, or three, or more, I don't remember, attended to her through a rhythm of siren screams. Someone said the words *torn* and *uterus*.

I squeezed her hand three times.

She only squeezed back once.

An hour later I sat in the waiting room between my in-laws. Lou Lou slept under a hospital blanket on a bank of chairs near me.

We waited. Waited. Waited for a smiling doctor to swing through the doors in triumph. Waited for life to reverse itself. Waited for Him to take a child and save a mother. Waited for the veil to return Emma Jane.

Hoped she was taking the long way.

There are sounds and words we do not forget.

"She is gone."

Ten
The Letter

My dear Emma Jane,

It is dawn and I am sitting in your rocking chair on the front porch. I am writing on a blank page in your journal, just in case you come for it. It's the tan cowhide journal with a cross and a dove stitched in white thread on the front. You've filled it almost halfway already this year. Why didn't I know you wrote so much or so often?

I promise I've only skimmed a few entries.

I have been here on the porch most of the night, waiting for the dream to end. I sit expecting you to appear in the orchard, walk toward me in the clothes you wore last night, shake my shoulders, tell me you were worried because I cried out in my sleep. But now as light fills the orchard I try to accept it. This is no dream, is it? Are you really dead and gone?

Sweet Lou Lou is on the couch inside. She cried herself to sleep with her head on my lap. She's in shock, I think. Your parents offered to take her to their house last night when we left the hospital, but I did not want to be alone on the orchard.

So why do I feel alone anyway?

If this is real, Emma Jane, how do I start this day without you? How will this day become another day, and another, and a week, and a season, and Christmas, and spring, and the last day of school, and a summer and a new harvest and a county fair?

Is it still our anniversary if you are not there? Does Lou Lou's recital happen without you? Does any of it happen without you standing by me?

What comes of the harvest we're in? Can I walk the rows and gather apples knowing you are not waiting for me on this same porch? What happens to the nights we wait for the men to go home and we walk row after row after row after row holding hands? Will I ever walk the rows again without smelling your sweetness in the air around me?

There have been only three women in my life. The mother I never met, you, and Lou Lou. She is still just a sweet little girl, but a beautiful woman in progress, no doubt. A future Emma Jane.

Mother is gone.

You are gone.

Lou Lou is left with me. And why? Why wouldn't yours be the lap she fell asleep on last night? What sort of God takes a mother and leaves a father alone with a daughter? And why? Why? For what?

Lou Lou needs you more than me, Emma Jane. Do you know that? Did God know that and not give it a thought? Why?

You know I am not afraid to try. I am not afraid. You have known me for long enough to know I do not fear what most men and boys fear. But I fear this. I fear my life without you. I fear Lou Lou's life without you. I am afraid she will suffer without your influence. And she will suffer with only mine, Emma Jane. She will surely suffer.

The man who drove the truck is home now in his bed by his wife. His wife is holding him, I imagine. He is telling her how lucky he is. She is praying and giving thanks to God and luck and a big safe truck. They are planning their tomorrows. When will the truck be fixed? Can you borrow another? Can you believe that pregnant woman died?

Was it a radio that distracted him? A spill? A cigarette? Something else?

He told the police he did not see her. He did not see the van. He thought we were parked too far into the road. All lies I'm sure. Why?

The orchard is brightening and you're still not here. So what. I keep scanning the trees anyway. Are you still near? Can there be a good-bye? Have I been worthy of it? Are you alone and waiting for some strange guide? Or was my mother there? Tim? Father? Anyone?

I think you're bound for whatever world takes angels and mothers.

Emma Jane Bevan, I pray my life will inch on somehow. But it will be broken, quiet, lonely. Alone without the only woman I have ever loved or who ever loved me.

I am leaving this journal by the others on the shelf in your room. Right where I found it last night and with your pen beside it.

There is nothing else for me now but calls and visitors and food I expect will fill the house by noon. Will this pain go when the food is gone?

If you see my father, my mother, Grandpa, or Tim, tell them each I miss them terribly.

Emma Jane, please help me.

God, if you're there, help me, too.

Love,
John

Eleven
August 28, 2008

W E buried them in a cemetery.
 I don't know why I didn't argue more forcefully with Emma Jane's parents, Bob and Michelle. As I knelt beside the sterile metal table that held her body that night in the emergency room, I had already pictured burying her in the orchard by my grandfather, father, and brother.

I could see a small grave there, too, for Willard.

But on August 28th, less than a week after I watched her eat strawberry-topped funnel cake from the top of the slide, we buried them both in Panorama Memorial Gardens in Strasburg. Emma Jane's parents, ever the accountants, had purchased family plots years earlier when they said the "prices were right."

Emma Jane was buried first in her favorite Sunday dress. I overheard others saying how peaceful and beautiful she looked. Not me. I thought she looked plastic. Like a wax mummy with a painted-on face. Like a CPR dummy. I didn't want to feel that way and I'd spent two days since first seeing her at the funeral home convincing myself it was the same gorgeous princess I'd married six years earlier.

But it wasn't.

Later Willard was lowered into the same hole with three feet of dirt separating them. His casket was so small it looked like the box my father had kept his favorite cowboy boots in. Smaller than the arms that carried it to the hole. Smaller than the flat brass-and-granite marker that later bore his name.

Smaller than an apple bin.

I cannot explain why some details are crisp and rich. Garlic mashed potatoes served by the Woodstock caterer Bob and Michelle hired. I sat in the exact middle of the front row. The colors in the stained glass window directly above the preacher, directly above the pulpit, directly over her casket. The limp, dead-fish handshake I got from Joshua Waits in the receiving line. The overdone smell of Michelle's perfume. The exact number of roses and carnations on Emma Jane's casket. The six fluffy tufts of hair on Willard's head—like dandelions in a dirt field. The soft, plush white outfit he wore, a baby shower gift from a friend. It was 0–6 months and far too big for Willard. *It buried him*, I thought.

Other moments and images are foggy, lost like the trucks behind the wavy glass of the firehouse on Court Street. Will the doors ever open?

Someone opened the service with a long, lovely prayer. Who? Was Scott's longtime girlfriend, April, there at his side? Had I been given the condolence books? Who closed the caskets after the private viewing? My mother-in-law slept at the orchard the night before and helped Lou Lou get ready for the day, but I don't remember the dresses either of them wore.

Emma Jane's best friend from high school sang a duet, "God Be with You Till We Meet Again," but I do not remember with whom she sang. I only remember that neither could sing by the time the piano played the final chords.

After the funeral, the long procession to Strasburg, the burial, the graveside prayer, the early dinner back at the church, after friends and family said good-bye and hugged Lou Lou and me a final time, I drove the two of us all the way back to the empty cemetery. We sat on the ground near the grave. The funeral home, Dellinger's, had disassembled the tent and placed the leftover funeral flowers on top of the fresh dirt.

Where else, when else does this happen? I thought. Rich and vibrant roses, carnations, greenery, all piled high on top of grave dirt. Red Virginia clay. A garden's worth of baby's breath mixed in.

The sun had set and night surrounded us, like the climax of a black-and-white movie with a single, poignant camera shot of colorful flowers.

Lou Lou held a stuffed turtle wearing a backpack she'd gotten at Fair Oaks Mall in Fairfax a month earlier. She'd named him Shell.

I held a white carnation by the stem and spun it.

Lou Lou unzipped Shell's backpack and removed the pink bunny she'd won at the county fair. She made it hop on a line between the dirt and grass.

Watching her was more painful than staring at the white polymer temporary markers stuck in the ground next to each other like small real estate or political campaign signs. They had black outlined crosses and said *In Memory of Emma Jane Elkington Bevan* and *In Memory of Willard John Bevan, Infant.*

I turned my back on her and memorized the graves around us. At some point I turned far enough to see Lou Lou again.

She was feeding grass to the stuffed rabbit. And though she was only a few feet away, it felt like miles.

Lou Lou caught my eyes and read an invitation to come closer. She picked up Shell and crawled on her hands and knees the short distance from her piece of ground to mine. She sat next to me and resumed feeding the rabbit.

I picked up the turtle and brushed a spot of dirt from its belly.

She looked up at me with vacant eyes that begged for guidance, a signal, a flash of reassurance.

But my eyes were vacant, too.

"I'm tired," I mumbled.

Lou Lou and Shell both nodded their tired heads in agreement.

Tears quickly began to drip from my bottom lashes and gather in a stream. I turned my head and wiped them on my sleeve.

When I looked back, Lou Lou was doing the same thing in the other direction.

Then, for the first of many times, the missed mile markers came rushing past me. Emma Jane wouldn't see Lou Lou's graduation from elementary, middle, and high school. She would miss her first date, first kiss, the night she was to give Lou Lou *the talk.*

Report cards. Driver's tests. Choir concerts. Field trips. Homecoming. Recitals. A wedding. A baby shower.

Lou Lou put her heavy head on my lap.

"No sleeping here, Lou. I'm tired, too." I stood up. "Let's go."

I looked down at Willard's marker as I stepped by. His list of missed mile markers overwhelmed me.

Twelve
First Day

THE men were on the orchard at 6:20 A.M.

We'd harvested eight thousand bushels of Ginger Golds in early August, but the real work now began. We still had forty-five acres of Red Delicious, Gala, Braeburn, and Granny Smith to pick and deliver to our retail accounts and a processor in Winchester.

"Mr. John, the men are ready."

I stood in my robe at the front door. "Of course. Start by the road, first row."

The man nodded and returned to the truck parked on the edge of the grass too close to the picket fence. He shouted directions in Spanish and five men spilled out of the quad cab truck. Another five hopped out of the bed. One drove the truck toward the back of the orchard, to pick up bins and picking bags, I presumed. The others began walking down the driveway to begin their ten-hour day.

I stood watching until the last man disappeared down the hill.

Lou Lou was still asleep.

It had been four days since the funeral and Lou Lou still hadn't started kindergarten. She'd missed a week already at Sandy Hook Elementary School.

I walked to her room and opened the door a crack. She clutched her pink bunny. I noticed Shell and his backpack had fallen on the floor at some point during the night. I slipped it under the covers next to her and rested his head on the pillow by hers.

I sat on the bedside.

"You start kindergarten today, Lou."

I looked around her room. No book bag. No outfit picked out and laid across her dresser the way Emma Jane would have done.

"You're ready today, right? If you need more time, that's okay, too."

I knew she wouldn't answer, but I also knew it might not have mattered even if she'd been awake. She hadn't said more than a few words since the accident. The doctor said it was normal, not to rush it, not to push her faster than she was ready.

Her grandparents had kept her over the weekend and said she hadn't spoken to them either. Mostly she watched *SpongeBob* and put things in her turtle's backpack. They'd wanted to keep her a few more days, *just to be safe*, they said. But I didn't know what they were keeping her safe from. So I picked her up Sunday night and drove through McDonald's on the way back to the orchard. She was asleep before we ever got to Middle Road.

"So you tell me, Lou. Just tell me whatever you want to do. I can take you today and introduce you to your teacher. Or you can wait another day. Or a week. Whatever you want."

I left her to sleep and crossed the hall to my own room. Emma Jane was everywhere. The wedding photo on the dresser. The pumpkin sweater she couldn't decide whether or not to take to the fair that night. It hung where she'd left it on the closet doorknob. The short bookshelf held her collection of journals, including the one I'd left the note in for her. The half-empty bottle of water on the nightstand by her side of the bed. Also on the nightstand sat the copy of *The Shack* she'd been reading to me at night. Our place in chapter thirteen was marked with a piece of thermal-paper-turned-bookmark she'd gotten at the hospital. A picture of Willard at twenty-one weeks.

I sat on the bed, picked up the book, stuck my finger where the bookmark was, and examined the photo. Five fingers. Five toes. One arrow pointed to the tiny heart. Another pointed to the evidence he was going to be a Willard and not a Stella. We'd decided on those names in the car on the way to the sonogram that day, and Emma Jane had squeezed my hand three times when the nurse pointed to what we could already see so clearly for ourselves. It was a he. And he would be Willard Bevan.

"Baby Willard," she'd whispered to me. I returned the black-and-white photo to its place in the book and the book to its place on the night-stand.

I scooted to my side of the bed and lay back. The last time I'd slept in it Emma Jane was beside me and my hands were under her pajama top feeling Baby Willard kick with both feet.

The couch had been my bed ever since, though I knew at some point I'd need to go home to our bed.

I pulled Emma Jane's pillow toward me and buried my nose in it. Then I pulled it against my chest and hugged it with my arms. It smelled exactly like I knew it would. An hour passed, but I did not sleep.

The TV turned on in the living room and I returned Emma Jane's pillow to its place.

"Good morning, Lou Lou." She was lying on the couch watching *Phineas and Ferb*. "How did you sleep?"

She didn't answer, but when I sat she switched ends of the couch and put her head on my lap. Later we ate Froot Loops and watched television until one of the pickers knocked on the door.

It was noon.

"We eat lunch now, yes?"

"Of course."

"Mr. John bring water?"

That was Emma Jane's job, I thought. "Of course, I'm sorry."

The man left and I asked Lou Lou if she wanted to help me fill the coolers with ice and water for the pickers.

She shook her head.

"Okay then."

I filled two coolers and tied them to a four-wheeler with bungee cords. I watched for a few minutes. Some of the men made eye contact and offered a shy wave. Others did not look at all. One actually poured his bag in a bin and walked over to me. He held open his arms and hugged me. His chest was soaked with sweat, and his hands and forearms left marks on the back of my T-shirt. *"Lo siento,"* he said, letting go of me.

I would have responded, but the gesture so surprised me I could only nod and give a closed-lip half-smile.

Back in the living room a few minutes later I found Lou Lou lying again on the couch, asleep and using Shell as a pillow. Bunny was leaning against the couch, sitting on Lou Lou's back, and looking very content watching *Caillou.*

So I spent the rest of the day watching *Caillou,* too.

Thirteen
Route 11

L OU Lou clung to me when she finally went to school for the first day of kindergarten.

Eventually though, her teacher, Ms. Silvious, coaxed her in, and two sweet girls were assigned to be her shadow.

"Have you ever had a shadow?" Ms. Silvious asked from her knees with her arms on Lou Lou's arms.

Lou Lou nodded.

"You have? Wonderful. Well now you're going to have *two*." She motioned for the two girls to approach the classroom doorway where our drop-off unfolded. "This is Gwyneth and Vanessa, and they're going to help you with whatever you need, okay?" She motioned for the girls to come even closer.

"I'm Vanessa," one of them said.

"I'm Gwyneth. You'll like Ms. Silvious, she's the best teacher ever."

Their smiles were so pure, so natural, I assumed they hadn't been told why Lou Lou might need a couple of ready-made friends.

I knelt in front of Lou Lou and we hugged each other with equal force for quite some time.

Finally I pulled free and looked straight into her eyes from a close distance. "Have a good day, darling. I'll see you after school out front, okay?"

Lou Lou didn't answer; she was whisked away by her shadows into the classroom and to a desk in a cluster with theirs.

"She'll be just fine, Mr. Bevan. I'll watch her closely. And the counselor will check in every day, too."

I thanked her and walked back to the truck.

I started the engine and kept a promise I'd made to myself on the first day of school Lou Lou missed. I pulled out of the school and drove toward Route 11. Then instead of turning right toward the orchard, I turned left toward Woodstock.

Left toward Maurertown.

Left toward Toms Brook.

Left toward the crash site.

A few miles later I approached fading skid marks and the remnants of two police flares someone had kicked to the shoulder. But I did not stop. I drove south another few miles to Toms Brook and turned around.

I passed by again, this time slower, and saw the carcass of the deer still in a heap in the clearing to my right. Seeing the scene for the first time was precisely as hard as I thought it would be.

I drove north back to Strasburg and parked in a convenience store lot. I went inside and bought the only gloves they had, a cheap pair of faux leather driving gloves. I also bought a small package of sunflower seeds and a 42-ounce Sprite. I politely asked for and was given an extra cup. Back inside the truck I popped seeds in my mouth and spit the shells in the cup. It was a habit Emma Jane wasn't fond of.

By the time I finished the drink, the ice had melted and the last ounces tasted more like water than soda. I drank it anyway, tossed the cup in a trash can by the front door, and used their restroom.

Back to the truck. I put a large palm full of seeds in my mouth, turned the ignition, started the AC, and leaned my head back against the headrest. I sucked the salt off each shell, bit it in two, let the seed fall to my tongue, and spat the shards of shell into the cup.

The seeds were gone. My mouth was dry. The sun was high in the sky. I went back into the store and bought a bottle of water.

"Everything alright?" the clerk asked.

I stared a moment at the older woman and her extra poufy bun hairdo.

"Sir?"

"I'm fine. Why?"

"Just asking. Looks like maybe you might be waiting for someone. Yeah?"

"No." I took my change and left. All the way back to the truck I wondered if she knew.

I started the ignition again and pulled to the entrance/exit of the parking lot. *The men could use my help at the orchard,* I thought.

I pictured Lou Lou sitting with her shadows. Probably at a lunch table. Lou Lou was no doubt picking at whatever they served today. And some of the kids had certainly heard about her mother. Were they asking her about it? *I should call the school,* I thought.

A Ford Explorer bearing the name of a sign company, Sound Design, drove past me and I remembered that Scott had suggested changing the name of the orchard from its generic longtime name, The Apple Orchard, to something in Emma Jane's memory. He even offered to handle the legal paperwork to make the change official. I'd agreed but not made any calls about changing signs or logos.

A car behind me honked. I waved an apology and pulled back onto 11 and in the direction of what I'd originally come for. I decided that if the car were too close to me when I reached the spot, I'd pass by once again and turn around farther down the road instead of slowing him down by pulling off the narrow two-lane road. But just before we reached the skid marks, the sedan had turned right and disappeared down a private driveway.

Again I pictured Lou Lou struggling through her first day, shy and reserved, uneasy, her stomach churning and aching. Wanting to be home. Wanting to be safe.

I crossed the double yellow line, right through the skid marks, and pulled off the left side of the road. My truck was so far off the road, another car could have parked at my side and still been safely beyond the white line marking the shoulder.

I removed the tag from the gloves and put them on. A deep breath. A drink of my water. A prayer, my first in at least a week. I left the truck and walked toward the deer.

He was covered in flies. So many it looked like hundreds buzzed around him in the air waiting for a clear spot and their turn. It was also obvious the ravaging buffet by other critters and birds had begun. The stench was horrid—thick, almost visible with the pollen in the humid valley air. I'd seen plenty of roadkill before, but never after being dead for so long.

I held it in as long as I could, even breathing through the collar of my shirt for a moment with my back to the animal, but eventually the rotting smell of deer flesh made me vomit Sprite and bits of sunflower seeds.

I judged by the size of what were likely his first set of small antlers that the deer was eighteen months to two years old. I hadn't hunted since Emma Jane and I were married, not because she didn't want me to, but because I preferred spending my free time with her. Still, I'd learned plenty at the side of my brothers during weekend hunting trips as boys.

There was no reason for it, and I was grateful no one had been driving by at that moment, but after wiping vomit from my chin I swore at the animal and kicked him in the side as hard as I could. Twice.

I grabbed the deer's back legs and pulled him out of the grassy clearing and to the edge of the woods. He was heavier than he looked, and I had to stop once for a minute to catch my breath. I made it to the tree line where I'd planned on leaving him, but when I got back to the truck and turned around, I could still see his bloated body. So I walked back and dragged him even farther into the trees and out of sight. I even covered him with brush and kicked some leaves over him. He was covered not out of respect, but because I didn't want to run the risk of seeing him ever again.

Walking away a second time, I realized I might have cried if the smell hadn't been so putrid.

From the bed of the truck I pulled a large rubber mallet I'd brought from the shed. I also pulled out two wooden crosses I'd made a few days earlier from a broken apple bin. One cross was larger, freshly painted white, and read simply *EJB 2008* in bold strokes of black paint. The other cross was much smaller. It was also white, but for reasons I could not explain, I'd chosen to leave it blank and without markings. Pure.

The bottom legs of the crosses had been sanded, by my own hand, into sharp points. But the ground near the road was filled with chunks of pavement and gravel and was still too hard to penetrate more than an inch or two. Instead I pounded Emma Jane's cross into the ground about five feet from the edge of the shoulder in the soft earth beneath the grass and weeds. It stood on a direct line between the spot the van had been hit and the dead yellow grass where the stunned deer had collapsed. I knew it didn't matter, but I paced it from the exact middle of the skid marks anyway. Twelve paces. Thirty-six feet.

I planted Baby Willard's cross to the right of Emma Jane's. Standing back and admiring it, I hoped that at the right time of day his cross would sit comfortably in the shadow of hers.

The harvest. The men. The house. The calls to return. Lou Lou's first day. All of it seemed farther off the road than I was as I sat behind the crosses and pulled every weed I could reach. So I just kept pulling. And soon I was memorizing the soundtrack of the site.

Cars whiz by. One honks. More cars. One needs muffler work. One has the distinctive sound of a German engine. Motorcycles blaze by in a gaggle. Now and then a car rolls to a near stop as it passes by, and sympathetic eyes seem to say something. One voice even calls, "God bless you," from an open window. In the trees behind me, crows call and flap over what must be lunch. A bike creeps by so slowly I hear the gears crank and the tires scratching on the loose bits of rock on the surface of the road.

I wanted to believe Emma Jane was there to appreciate the soundtrack with me.

I know now she wasn't.

Fourteen
Kidnapped

"YOU'RE coming with me."

I was on the couch and Scott was standing over me with a cup of water. "Let's go."

"I can't, I've got to be here when Lou Lou gets home." I covered my head with the pillow.

"I've got you covered. I talked to Bob and Michelle already, and they'll pick her up from school and keep her overnight. She's in good hands. Now get up."

"Whttimist?" I asked through the pillow.

"What?"

"Whttimist?"

"John, you're going to have to move the pillow."

I did, and my face was greeted by bright morning light and a cup of ice-cold water. "Come on, Scott, how old are we?" I sat up and spit on his shoes the mouthful of water I'd captured.

"Today we're teenagers again."

"Shouldn't you be working?" I asked.

Scott sat by me on the couch and rested his feet on the coffee table between us and the television. He slid a bowl of soggy cereal aside with his foot. "I might ask you the same question."

"I'm supervising. The guys are out there."

"Supervising from the couch?"

"I worked hard yesterday, cut me some slack."

"How did Lou Lou get to school?"

"Same way we did. The yellow thing with wheels."

"And then you came back in and went back to bed?"

"Technically back to the couch, but yeah, I dozed off. What is this? You drove all the way out here to harass me?"

"Harass is a strong word. Let's say it's me checking on my little brother. I'm kidnapping you for some fun. You need it. Now go get in the shower." He swung his legs around and pushed me with his feet until I got off the couch. "And take your time, you smell terrible."

"Since you asked so nicely." I tossed him the remote on my way out of the room.

Fifteen minutes later I returned to find him

doing dishes. "Come on, man, you don't need to be my maid."

"Someone does. This place is a mess." He washed the last two plates and when I turned my back to put the Honeycomb back in the cereal cupboard, he flicked the back of my thigh with a damp dish towel.

"Sweet mother!" I grabbed my leg with one hand and a smelly washcloth with the other. "Bring it." I twirled the rag in front of me like a lasso and we circled each other around the kitchen.

"I'll eat you alive, John. You know this to be true."

" 'You know this to be true'? You sound like an attorney."

"I *am* an attorney." He passed by the sink and picked up a second weapon, a washcloth I could smell from across the kitchen when he whipped it through the air. "This thing smells rotten. Don't you own a washer?" He leapt at me and tried to flick me with both cloths at the same time.

I tried to grab the longer one in the air, but it flicked my palm. "Ahhhhh! That's gonna leave a mark."

"That's the idea." He lunged at me again, but this time I timed it better and grabbed the end of the dishcloth with my left hand and flicked his stomach with my own washcloth. We tugged back and forth and swung wildly at one another with the other cloths. At one point we found ourselves on opposite sides of the kitchen table, arms stretched across, still playing tug-of-war and whipping our respective rags at one another's body parts in search of the winning welt.

"Truce," I said. "The cap is barely on that milk." A gallon of 2% sat just a few inches from the edge of the table on his side.

"You'll come with me?"

"Where?"

"Wherever I say. It's a kidnapping."

"When do you have to go back into the city?"

"Tonight, tomorrow morning, whenever I want."

I saw him relax his grip slightly on the dish towel. I ripped it from his hands and in the same motion flicked the back of his hand as hard as I could.

"Nice!" he bellowed and shook his wrist. As he did, his hip bumped the table hard, the milk teetered, he quickly reached out to steady it but instead knocked it to the side. The milk splashed out and began gurgling from the jug onto the table, racing across the uneven surface to the tile floor.

I laughed. Then I looked at Scott and saw drops of milk on one of his eyebrows and laughed harder.

Scott laughed, too, right until he realized someone was watching through the back door. He gestured with his head. One of my pickers was standing at the door smiling. "I got this," Scott said, still giggling more than he probably realized.

"Thanks," I said. "More towels under the sink, if they're clean."

I stepped outside.

"Hello, Mr. John," he said in nearly unintelligible English.

"What's up?"

"Gas. For trucks. Two trucks. No gas." He held up two fingers, as if "two" had been the most difficult word he'd used.

"Wait." I went inside and found one of the prepaid gas cards I'd bought to prepare for the harvest. Back outside I handed it to him, he shook my hand, smiled, and walked back to one of the two trucks.

Inside, Scott was on his hands and knees wiping up milk from underneath the table. I picked up one of the washcloths draped over a chair, twisted it, and considered leaving a welt on his backside that he'd never forget.

"Don't even think about it," he said. "You called truce."

"I can't believe you don't trust me," I said, circling behind him. "That's offensive." The sound of the rag whipping and flipping him on the right back pocket of his slacks was probably heard across the orchard. "Now it's a truce."

We finished cleaning the kitchen.

I started a load of laundry, including almost every towel in the house.

Scott tossed a barbeque sandwich, a plastic container of coleslaw, and a leftover bucket of fried chicken into the trash can outside.

As we drove off the orchard I asked if he wanted to go by the crosses in the orchard before we left.

"Not today. Let's go have some fun."

I stopped at the bottom of the driveway. "Where to?"

"Winchester."

We sped along the back roads and talked about his girlfriend, April, his new condo in Ballston, and the terrible season the Nationals had in their expensive new ballpark on the banks of the Anacostia.

I wanted to offer to take him by the crosses on Route 11. *Will he want to see the place they died? I thought. Will it matter to him the way it matters to me?* He broke the silence before I did.

"Did I tell you about the case I'm working on now?"

"Don't think so."

"Got handed off to me by one of the partners."

I began listening more to the road than to him.

"Dispute over a website . . . Filed suit . . . Wrong company . . . name . . . Fees . . . Silly . . . Head . . . Platter . . . You listening, John?"

"Yeah." I was glad he didn't quiz me.

"Anyway, interesting case. Glad I'm on the honorable side of it."

We arrived in Winchester.

"Where to, Johnnie Cochran?"

"I was thinking a matinee, then lunch, then maybe hit some golf balls at Apple Valley. Maybe even hit their par-three course."

"This is my kind of kidnapping."

We saw *Pineapple Express*, a movie Emma Jane would have never watched with me. I don't know if I laughed because the movie was funny, or because I just needed to laugh, but when Scott asked me how long it had been since I'd laughed so hard, I couldn't remember.

"Too long, obviously," he said.

We laughed our way through a late lunch at a Chinese buffet. Scott told me things with April were getting serious.

"How serious?"

"Ring serious," he answered.

"Really?"

"She might be the one."

"I'm happy for you, Scott. I really am." I was. It felt good to be happy for him, even if the conversation reminded me of the riverbanks of the Shenandoah and the day Emma Jane said yes and let me twirl her in the air.

We drove to the driving range in Stephens City and shared a large bucket of balls. Then Scott paid for us to play the short nine-hole, par-three course. His tee shot on the first hole landed eight feet from the hole. Mine landed eight feet in front of us.

"It's been a while," I said, swinging at my ball a second time and sending it burning five feet above the fairway toward the target. It stopped on a hill behind the green.

"Me, too. I thought being a lawyer would give me the perfect lifestyle for golf. What was I thinking?"

"That a six-figure salary beat picking apples in the heat?"

"Yes, but grunts like me don't play much golf. It's a lot harder than I thought."

"Father told you it would be."

"Everyone did."

We walked so comfortably from one hole to another. No hurry. No concerns. No one behind us; the course was practically empty.

Scott played well. I played like someone who'd never played golf before, even though I had taken lessons from Scott a few times through the years.

"Thanks for this, by the way."

"Forget it. It's just money."

"I mean for all of it. Lunch, golf, dragging me off the couch."

"Come on, forget about it. You needed this. I probably did, too."

I butchered the eighth hole, hitting three balls in

the water to the left before finally hitting one on the cart path to the right. I think I got a thirteen. Scott pared with a six-foot putt that nearly circled the entire cup before falling in. "I meant to do that," he said.

"Uh-huh." I grabbed the ball from the cup before he could and chucked it into the same pond I'd hit mine in. But while I was admiring the splash, he goosed me with his putter.

"When was the last time you played?" Scott asked on the ninth tee.

"I played with Emma Jane here once on a date night after Lou Lou was weaned. So four years ago? Something like that?"

"Oh yeah." He laughed. "You borrowed my clubs and bent my last putter."

Scott teed off with a pitching wedge on the downhill hole and his ball landed on the back fringe, far from the hole location in the front right quarter of the green.

I took his nine iron—we'd been sharing his set all day—and took a practice swing before standing over the ball and clunking it halfway to the green, barely off the ground. To my surprise, it bounced high off a mound and caught speed as gravity and a tightly mowed fairway pulled it toward the front of the green.

"Watch it," Scott said when the ball trickled through the fringe in a line for the hole. "That could go in." He paused. "That could go in!"

I watched and silently willed it along.

"Go!" he yelled, and the ball continued tracking toward the flag stick. "Go, go, go!" he yelled louder, and a group standing on the first tee watched with interest.

But, as I feared, the ball ran out of steam a few inches from the cup and came to a stop on the lip.

"You've got to be kidding me!" Scott shouted. "That close!"

I shrugged my shoulders and dropped the club in his bag. "That's life."

Scott heaved the bag over his shoulder and slapped me on the back. "You sure took the long way, but you got it there." He turned his head back toward the green as we stepped off the tee box and began descending the hill. "I can't believe you—"

The ball was gone.

"John, what happened to your ball?"

I took off running down the hill, careless, laughing, nearly falling on my face, caught momentarily in a different reality than what awaited me at home.

Scott followed, clubs banging and clanging in the bag behind him. We got to the hole at the same time and leaned over slowly.

The ball was in it.

You could have driven a truck through our gaping jaws.

"You just got an ace," Scott said. "Unbelievable."

I reached in and pulled out the ball, holding it with two fingers and staring through it. "I just got a hole in one."

"I've been playing golf since high school. Never had an ace. Never." He slugged me on the bicep. "You are the luckiest guy alive."

I smiled at him. And for an instant, barely a blink, I couldn't wait to get home to tell Emma Jane. But as quickly as the ace happened, the ball was out of the hole, back in Scott's golf bag, and Emma Jane was still dead.

Fifteen
First Visit

THE routine was comfortable.

Lou Lou missed the bus and I dropped her off at school without needing to walk her in. Often one or both of her shadows would linger by the buses until they saw our truck pull up. I hadn't asked, but it seemed she didn't need me anymore as an escort.

Sometimes I stopped for a snack on the way. Sometimes I brought one from home. Sometimes I talked to the pickers on my way off the orchard. Sometimes I pretended to be on my cell phone and drove past them if they made eye contact.

Sometimes I went to the cemetery first to visit

their graves. Sometimes I didn't. But I always ended up at the side of Route 11 next to two crosses in a clearing. Each visit made the night clearer, the memories more crisp. Watching the sun move across the crosses reminded me how they'd gotten there. I felt closer to Emma Jane and Willard at the place where they left this world than the ground they lay in.

Two weeks had passed since my first visit to the crosses and I'd made ten more since, each lasting longer than the previous. A couple of the visits should have ended when thunderstorms crashed into the valley and the rain clouds exploded over me. But they didn't. I sat and listened even harder for Emma Jane's voice until the rain passed.

It's okay, John, I don't mind. As long as I'm off my feet. We can take the long way for Lou Lou.

One afternoon I was so late getting home to meet Lou Lou at the bottom of the driveway that one of the pickers had walked her up the hill and put her to work on the sorting table behind the house. The man stood next to her and helped her recognize which apples were not good enough to be packaged. Twenty years ago that man was my father. Now it was a Mexican I didn't know.

Another time I was even later. She'd gone inside, found something to eat, and drifted to sleep on the couch with the television on. I was grateful she hadn't called Emma Jane's parents.

They hadn't mentioned it yet, but I feared Bob

and Michelle had driven by and seen me there. Maybe that's why I felt the need to start parking farther down the road and walking to the site, hoping to draw less attention without my truck parked roadside.

One of the trips came after school. I'd asked Lou Lou in the morning if she was ready to join me, and she nodded yes. We stopped by Rite Aid and Lou Lou picked out a red metal race car for Baby Willard and a package of three rainbow hair bands for her mother. They weren't what Emma Jane would have ever worn, but as she pulled them from a $1 rack, Lou Lou looked convinced her mother would have loved them. I picked out a gift, too, a six-inch ceramic angel. We also bought an orange pumpkin balloon just because it was already blown up and tied to the magazine rack by the register. Lou Lou didn't take her eyes off it all the way from Rite Aid to the site.

With the windows up and the radio off, I could hear Lou Lou's breathing become more labored when we neared the clearing. I didn't want her walking alongside the road, so I pulled off at the clearing and circled all the way behind the crosses on the grass. Out her window she stared at the spot where the van had sat. She'd not been back since, and I wondered if her senses were keen enough to know.

They were.

I got out of the truck and walked around to her

side. She was crying as I helped her out and she immediately grabbed me around the waist. Her little chest heaved in and out with the kind of deep anguish a child should never know.

In time she calmed, and I asked her if she wanted to go home. She shook her head emphatically and retrieved the balloon from the backseat of the truck. She also removed the gifts we'd purchased from the Rite Aid bag and took baby steps toward the crosses. She looked back at me as if to ask, *Here?*

"Anywhere," I said.

She handed the balloon to me and I tied it to Baby Willard's cross. She set the car on the ground next to it and the ceramic angel and hair bands next to Emma Jane's. She traced the initials and year with her index finger, and I realized she hadn't seen the crosses up close. She'd only watched me make them from the safety of a rocking chair on our front porch at the orchard.

I invited her to sit, but she didn't.

So I did, and I watched her walk back to the spot where the deer had died. The evidence was gone, the grass recovered, what remained of the carcass off in the woods, but she'd stopped at the same spot where she'd knelt that night and prayed.

She knelt again, but unlike the night a deer and an inattentive redneck killed my wife and baby, I did not run to her side.

I watched.

Lou Lou's mouth appeared to be moving, and her palms were together in front of her, chin rested on top of extended fingers. In the clearing, in the sun, in front of two crosses and from my vantage point, she could have been a tragic painting.

I've wondered what Lou Lou said during that private time at the site. During her prayers in the cemetery, which I had overheard more than once, she talked about missing Mom and wondering what Baby Willard would have looked like. *Would he have liked cars? Tractors? Puzzles? Car rides?* she asked. *Would he have liked me?*

Now I wondered if it was different at the site. Was she praying to God or talking to them? Was she reporting to her mother on how she was doing? How I was doing? How the orchard was doing?

Or was she simply saying she was sorry, over and over and over again?

Sixteen
The Cross Gardener

THE harvest was slowly winding down. I'd not picked a Gala, Golden, or Red Delicious yet. In fact, I hadn't picked a single apple since we finished harvesting the Ginger

Golds in early August, weeks before Emma Jane and the baby were killed. Only the Braeburns were left to pick, and the men seemed to be getting along fine.

I wasn't picking. I wasn't sorting. I wasn't packing. I wasn't even delivering; I'd taken an offer from another orchard to handle my accounts. My responsibilities had been reduced to taking coolers of ice water every morning to whatever row the men started on. And I didn't always remember to do that.

Instead of working alongside the pickers, I sat on the porch every night as the sun set and waited for a report I didn't care much about. But my brother was calling nearly every night to check on me, and it was important to at least sound engaged in the work of the orchard.

The man responsible for finding and organizing the workers that year visited me every evening and relayed their progress. I did not remember his name then; I still don't. He might have been Miguel. He looked like a Miguel.

One evening after I'd spent much of the afternoon at the crosses, he and another worker pulled up in one of the two orchard trucks. I hadn't had time yet to paint the new name, Emma Jane's Orchard, on the side. But every time I saw a truck coming or going I reminded myself to get it done for her.

The driver pulled up through the gravel and

parked with the two front tires on my grass by the fence, just as he and others had done since I was five and still learning my way around the orchard. But I'd decided last time I saw it that I wouldn't let it happen again.

I stood and charged down the porch steps. "Seriously, Miguel? On my grass? Again?" I was either talking too fast or using words neither understood. Both men looked confused. I pointed at the tires. "Off the grass! Now. Off." I walked to the driveway and kicked gravel in their direction. "Driveway. Trucks. Get it?"

"Sorry, sorry," the driver said. He hopped in the truck and without shutting the door put it in reverse and backed up off the grass. "Sorry, Mr. John." He stepped out of the truck and put both hands up in a defensive pose.

I muttered a term that Emma Jane would have put me on the couch a week for using. It was just a word, but I knew it was an ugly stereotype. And if Father had heard me, it would have killed him.

Up the steps and into the house I marched. But before the door shut behind me I'd already whispered, "I'm sorry." If only they'd been alive to be disappointed.

I didn't get a report that day.

The next morning I woke up late, which meant I woke Lou Lou up late, too, and had missed the bus. I rushed her through dressing and handed her two stale donuts as we ran out the door. I sped her to the elementary school and cursed when I saw the empty parking lot.

"It's Saturday, isn't it?"

She didn't answer. But when I looked down at her in the passenger's seat, she nodded once and tried to smile.

"Want to visit the crosses and the cemetery?"

This time she shook her head—twice.

"Grandma's?"

I didn't need to wait for an answer; I knew she'd be content there for the day. I drove to Bob and Michelle's and was relieved to see both cars in the driveway. "You need me to come in?"

"No."

The word was so soft I wouldn't have known what she'd said if I hadn't seen her lips move. "Okay, see you later today. Have fun."

Michelle watched me from the open front door and tossed me a wave, but I pretended not to see.

I drove off toward Route 11.

I parked in my usual spot and walked along the left shoulder to the empty clearing. But it wasn't empty.

A man knelt beside Emma Jane's cross with his back to the road.

I stood, confused, on the side of Route 11. I looked left and right for others. We were alone.

I looked back at the man. He dipped a small paintbrush in a can of paint and brushed it along the thin edge of the top of the cross.

"May I help you?" I said, approaching.

No response.

"Hello?" I circled behind, the crosses now between us. "Excuse me?"

"I'm sorry," he said. "I must not have heard you."

"I guess not." I stood a little straighter. "What are you doing?"

"I'm just touching this one up, if you don't mind."

I did, but I couldn't have explained why if he'd asked. "Who are you?"

He ran the brush a final time along the small flat top of the vertical board in the cross. Then he stood. He was my height, probably a few years older, dark hair parted carefully like an altar boy. He wore a short-sleeved white button-down dress shirt and casual but crisp khaki pants. His right hand had paint on it. "I'm new to the Valley."

"I'm John and these are my wife's and son's crosses. You with the county?"

"Oh no." He laughed.

"Funeral home?"

"Neither, John."

"Then who are you?"

"I'm just a guy trying to help when I can."

I looked at his off-brand paint can. "Why are you painting my wife's cross?"

"This is for your wife?"

"Yes. And that small one is for my son."

"I'm sorry to hear that. I've been down the road and seen you before. My condolences."

"Thanks. But you didn't tell me why you're painting them."

He looked down at them. "They needed it?" It wasn't obvious whether it was an excuse or a question.

I had to admit, though not to him, I'd thought of touching them up myself. The alternating summer sun and rain had aged the crosses faster than the mere passage of a month. I stood my ground, quietly, invited more.

"This is what I do. I care for crosses and memorials like these."

"What? Why?"

"Why not?"

"What's your name?"

"My friends call me Cross Gardener. Just a nickname, of course."

"Cross—?"

"Gardener. Yeah, I know, very strange. It's because I tend to crosses, roadside crash sites like yours, mostly. It's kind of my thing." He raised his right hand as if taking an oath. "I promise I'm not some crackpot. This is just something that's—well—important to me."

"Why haven't I seen you before?"

"Just because you haven't seen me, doesn't mean I haven't been around. Besides, you know how many memorials like this there are in the Valley?"

Fair, I thought. I crossed my arms across my chest. "Well I do appreciate your concern. But I'll tend to these two. They're mine."

He smiled. "You wouldn't take my joy away, would you, John?"

I might, yes. I'm not sure how long I stared into the woods to the spot where I'd dragged the deer.

"John? You alright?"

"It's all a little weird, don't you think?" I looked back to the road. "How did you even get here?"

"Walked."

"From where?"

He pointed north.

"You walk everywhere?"

"It's a big Valley." It was his turn to look to his left and right. Then he whispered, "I live with my mother." He winked and put a finger over his closed mouth. "She gets me around. Today she left me down the road on the way to work."

I looked down at Emma Jane's and Willard's crosses. "Whatever then. As you can plainly see, these two crosses here are in fine shape. Maybe your time is better spent on older ones."

"Perhaps. But don't they all deserve to look fresh? To look cared for?"

I suppose so.

We stood without speaking for what felt like an awkward eternity, but the man's eyes never left me. Then he simply leaned down and picked up his paintbrush and can. "I'd love to stay, John, but I've got to get going. Saturdays are busy, you know. See you around sometime?"

"Maybe so."

The man smiled, turned his back slowly, walked from the crosses to the shoulder of the road and turned left, south down Route 11 toward Toms Brook.

I waited a moment before following his path to the edge of the road. A piece of me expected to see him vanish, like a scene in a movie, just a vision of my grief. But there he was, now fifty yards away, walking down the side of the road swinging a can of white paint in one hand and a paintbrush in the other. There he was—this man the Cross Gardener—as real as I, marching on toward some other roadside memorial.

I wondered what sins he was painting away.

Seventeen
Sunday Circuit

T HE circuit always started at the orchard.

There, on the highest point, were buried three good men and three crosses made from the wood of an apple bin and painted white.

Grandpa Bevan, Father, and Tim.

One killed by age and hard work. One killed by

cigarettes and stupidity. The other by stupidity and the Atlantic Ocean.

I walked in my baggy shorts and pizza-stained T-shirt out the back door of the house, through the gate in the fence, up the hill, past rows of trees picked clean, all the way to the clearing.

I sat at the three crosses. One Father made for Grandpa. Another he made for Tim. One I made for Father. The scene was familiar, so circular. So were the feelings of longing.

So were the words. "What's wrong with me?"

They never spoke back and I never stayed long. I walked back down the hill, through the gate, into the house, through the kitchen, picked up my keys by last night's pizza box, called Lou Lou from the living room, walked out the front door, passed through the other gate, opened the door to the truck, and waited.

Lou Lou always followed closely behind. She climbed into the front seat of the truck, despite knowing she was still too small to be up front. Emma Jane would never have allowed Lou Lou to ride up front if we were driving off orchard property.

I dropped her off at her grandparents' house for church and promised her I'd go next week. "I'm just not ready for church, Lou. And when I do go, I want to go back to our regular church, not Grandma and Grandpa's. Is that going to be okay?"

"Uh-huh."

"Lou, do you feel better when you go to church with Grandma and Grandpa?"

She shrugged her shoulders.

"Then you don't have to go. Come with me if you like."

But by then Michelle was always walking toward me, waving and inviting me in.

"Back tonight," I called. "Errands. Thanks."

Lou Lou watched over her shoulder as Michelle led her in the house. Soon she'd dress her in one of the outfits they'd bought after Emma Jane died to have on hand for occasions like this.

She'd worn all of them already.

Then began the circuit. I bought flowers at the Food Lion in Strasburg, the only Sunday option, and drove to the cemetery. I placed the flowers over her grave and always noted how the dead ones disappeared. One day I'd tell my in-laws I didn't mind if the flowers stayed longer.

After a short stay I circled back to the Route 11/81 interchange where on my sixteenth birthday a police report told me my mother was killed in winter weather.

There was no cross to visit. No memorial of any kind. Not even skid marks to stop my heart. But I knew she left me and I'd been born somewhere in that quarter-mile stretch just south of the exit.

The very first time I made my Sunday circuit I just drove down the road and imagined where the spot might have been. But after another week or two, I parked in the Burger King parking lot and actually walked along the road. I stopped every ten paces or so and listened for sirens.

Eventually I walked back to the truck and jumped on 81 south to Woodstock. I got off the exit, turned left on 42, left again on Ox, and left into the fairgrounds. When the gate was closed, I parked at the opening and walked in.

It didn't matter that the fair had been gone for over a month, I still saw the Zipper rising high and spinning its giddy, screaming riders. The Ferris wheel was there, too, circling the Valley sky. I thought of a young couple kissing for the first time when their basket was at the highest possible point, out of view from teasing friends or worried parents below.

The tractor pull was still going on in front of a packed grandstand. An emcee with a local country station made announcements over a PA system so loud it could be heard at the town park and tennis courts a mile away.

Since it was the opening Saturday of the fair, it was also Family Fun Day. That meant the annual Greased Pig Contest was drawing its usual healthy crowd. Lou Lou said she wasn't quite ready to participate, but she watched every second and critiqued the techniques of the young competitors. The Seed-Spitting Competition was also popular, and Emma Jane said she would have won the Rolling Pin Toss if she hadn't been pregnant.

"Next year," she said. "Next year I'll show them."

No she wouldn't.

The smells were even easier to recall. Lou Lou and I watched the 4-H Hog and Lamb Weigh-in. Emma Jane watched, too, but only until the wind shifted and blew the stall smells right across her nose.

It took me about a half hour to walk the grounds and relive the fair. No one ever bothered me. I stayed until I could hear Emma Jane whispering that her feet and back hurt. Then I wandered back to the truck and retraced the path to Route 11.

Driving down Main Street I passed some members of Emma Jane's book club sitting outside at Woodstock Café. The light was red, and, with three cars in front of me, I was stuck sitting directly across from the women at their outdoor table. They waved, called my name, and unfortunately, we made eye contact. I had no choice but to nod a hello. They had to notice that I hadn't shaved in weeks or had a haircut since the funeral. Or worse, that I hadn't returned any of their calls. *You should be embarrassed*, I thought.

I wasn't.

The light changed and I didn't look back. A block later I passed the movie theatre and felt guilty that I couldn't remember the last movie I'd seen there with Emma Jane. I was certain it was Bargain Night Monday, but could only hope that next time I drove past the film's title would find its way back to my mind.

I passed Ben Franklin and smiled when I saw the canoe standing upright on the sidewalk in front of Blue Canoe Crew at the end of the shopping center. Emma Jane's favorite shirt came from that shop; I'd given it to her on the Fourth of July to wear to the fireworks. It was the largest size they had and it stretched tight across her belly. I bought a matching one for Lou Lou. Both said, *If Found Please Return to the Shenandoah Valley.*

Lou Lou was wearing hers out.

Emma Jane's was sitting in a drawer at home.

No one loved canoeing the Shenandoah River quite like my Emma Jane Bevan. I prefer to think it was because I proposed on its banks, but she said she loved it because it reminded her of God. Powerful. Constant. Giving. Forgiving.

I continued north through Maurertown and slowed down at the park where we celebrated Lou Lou's fifth birthday with a moon bounce and a chocolate Texas sheet cake so big it nearly covered an entire picnic table. The table next to it held her birthday spoils. Clothes, books, and a Treasury Bond from the grandparents. Games, DVDs, and stuffed animals from her uncle Scott. A dress from Emma Jane that she'd made herself at night after putting Lou Lou to bed. The birthday girl liked it so much she insisted on running up to the park shelter with the restrooms and changing into it. Emma Jane cried when she sauntered back down to the party pavilion looking like a princess.

I drove on to Toms Brook.

Lou Lou should be asleep in the backseat of the van with a turtle named Shell and the pink bunny.

Emma Jane should be at my side with her head against the glass, resting comfortably.

That Sunday, like every other, as I approached the site I wondered where the deer had come from. Was he alone? Scared? Was he chasing something? Lost from his family? Had he been thrown into our path that night by his own desire to escape danger and survive? Did he hear us? Did he see us, even after I'd thumped him hard with the front of our gray Honda Odyssey?

What if he'd hesitated, just a second, on the side of the road, or been a half step faster?

What if we hadn't hit him?

I wouldn't have stopped.

Lou Lou wouldn't have gotten out.

I wouldn't have gone after her in the clearing.

Emma Jane wouldn't have been sitting alone in the van on the shoulder, and the van wouldn't have been there anyway.

Why did I ask her to stay? What if I'd asked

her to come with me to comfort our daughter? What if I'd thought to take advantage of a moment that would have bonded us, not torn us apart?

I closed my eyes and imagined all three of us gathered around the dying deer. Emma Jane would have held both our hands. She might have led a prayer and acknowledged a teaching moment provided by fate. It was to be a positive slice of Lou Lou's life she'd never forget.

Except it wasn't.

What if? What if I'd stopped for one single moment, no more, and considered the danger of leaving my pregnant wife on the side of the road in a parked car at dark?

The truck that hit her would have swerved into an empty van, or perhaps off the road and into the clearing. Or into the trees. Or he might have easily corrected back onto the road and driven on to whatever trashy trailer park he lived in.

But what if his truck had overcorrected, tipped, burned, exploded into a ball of fire seen all the way from the fairgrounds ten miles south?

There would be one cross instead of two, it would have his name on it, not hers, and I wouldn't even notice it.

I certainly wouldn't spend every Sunday visiting it.

Eighteen
Breakfast

I T was a teacher workday across Shenandoah County.

I had no idea what that meant, other than school was out that Tuesday and Lou Lou was home for the day. We slept much later than normal, and Lou Lou almost smiled when I offered to take her to breakfast.

I took the bowl of Cap'n Crunch she'd already poured herself and dumped it in the sink.

Lou Lou's eyes were big and interested.

"We don't waste food, normally, but this is a special occasion. Okay?

"You pick," I said. "I just need to eat something besides cereal."

She rolled her eyes up toward the ceiling and considered the options, just the way Emma Jane used to. She even grabbed her chin with her index finger and thumb, a wonderful and subconscious impression of her mother. But like so often since the accident, she didn't actually answer the question. Or say anything at all.

"Go get him. I'll wait."

She disappeared down the hall to her room and

returned with Shell, her turtle. The soft green creature with the backpack had become her speech pal. He spoke for her when she did not want to—or couldn't—speak for herself.

"Ready?"

She raised Shell's right hand.

Yes.

"Alright. Here are the choices."

She looked at me with unusual energy in her eyes.

"McDonald's."

No. Shell raised his left hand.

"Cracker Barrel."

No.

"Donuts."

Eh. She shrugged and raised both his hands.

"Hi Neighbor Restaurant? You love their pancakes."

No, Shell said.

"Waffle House?"

A toothy smile and a stuffed right arm went high in the air.

I must have stared too long because she pulled on my hand and her crinkled brow asked if I was okay.

I was.

In fact, at that moment I felt more okay than I had in weeks. I'd waited for this day. The day I passed a switch in the track that sent me on a better direction. "Let's go have an adventure."

The closest Waffle House was twelve miles north up 81 in Stephens City. Just before I pulled onto Middle Road at the bottom of the driveway I hit the brakes and asked Lou Lou to hop in the back of the quad cab.

"I know you don't like it, but it's dangerous on the highway."

She climbed over the seat and I swatted her fanny.

"Thanks, Lou." I drove on to our first breakfast out together since burying the rest of our family. I felt strong, or at least strengthened. Upheld. I was trying.

We rode in quiet—comfortable quiet—until traffic slowed just past the Middletown exit. We went from sixty-five miles per hour to thirty-five to stopped in less than a mile.

"It's probably just construction," I said, looking at Lou Lou in the rearview mirror.

She had her hands in her lap, fingers interlocked, tips white.

"It's always busy in the mornings, Lou, you just never see it because you're at school. This is rush hour. Lots of folks head up to Winchester every day. I bet you a waffle they're paving the road up there."

She pulled Shell onto her lap and folded her arms around him.

"Want to sing our song?" I knew she wouldn't, but she couldn't help but listen.

"Once there was a prairie dog,
Bobby was his name.
He liked to play hopscotch,
it was his favorite game."

In the mirror I saw her lips move along with the words to the silly song we'd made up on a road trip when she was just three.

"One day in the wintertime,
he went outside to play.
The snow covered his hopscotch court,
it was a very sad day."

I sang the third verse in the goofy opera voice Emma Jane used to love. She'd said it sounded like a dying cartoon wolf.

"When the winter turned to spring,
the snow did melt away.
Bobby did find his hopscotch court,
it was a happy day."

Lou Lou smiled in the backseat.
I think Shell was smiling, too.
"That's a terrible song, isn't it?"
Lou Lou gave me a playful dirty look and Shell raised his left hand. *No.*
I rolled down my window and breathed in the thin fall morning air. Leaning my head out the

window gave me a view of nothing but eighteen-wheelers. "I'll take a quick look. Stay here." I began to push open my door but abruptly turned to face her. "Did you hear me? Stay here. Do not leave this truck under any circumstances."

I didn't mean to frighten her. The irony was hateful. Her look distinctive, like a deer in the headlights. She raised Shell's right hand halfway.

On the shoulder of the highway I stood with three other curious and equally impatient drivers.

The scene ahead was not construction.

We saw at least two ambulances and one fire truck, with one more racing south and pulling across the median separating north and southbound traffic.

"I hope no one is hurt," one of the gawkers said.

"Doesn't look good," said another.

"No, not good at all," said a younger man in a black dress shirt and metallic silver tie. "This is so lame." He rubbed and pulled down on his goatee. "I'll never make it to work."

I looked back at Lou Lou. She'd slid across the backseat and was reading me intently through the glass, her eyes wide and worried.

Then came the hyper flicker of rotors in the sky.

A helicopter glided into view from the east and appeared to land north of the accident on the empty highway.

It only took a few seconds for me to get back in the truck, put it in four-wheel drive, bounce across the median to my left, and squeal into the southbound rubbernecking traffic. A black Honda del Sol honked and swerved past us.

"How about McDonald's?" I did not look back to see what Shell thought.

A few minutes later we exited at Route 11 in Strasburg, pulled into the drive-thru, ordered breakfast in a bag, and ate on the way to my in-laws.

"Hi, Michelle." I stood at the front door holding Lou Lou's orange juice.

She stood near me eating the final bite of a greasy hash browns and wiping her hands on her pajama bottoms.

Michelle watched her with a hand over her mouth.

"I know it's short notice, but could Lou Lou hang out with you today?"

"Go wash your hands, dear," Michelle said. "Go on." She stepped aside and Lou Lou scooted past her with Shell safely under her arm.

"I know, Michelle—"

"Wait, John. I've got a very busy schedule today. And you've got a parent-teacher conference this afternoon. Did you forget?"

"No, of course not." Sure I had. "I was wondering if you could—"

Her hand stopped me. "John. You need to go."

I dug my hands in the pockets of my dirty jeans.

"I can't today, Michelle. Please. Today just isn't good."

Michelle didn't need to tell me what she was thinking. I read her almost as well as I'd read Emma Jane, and Michelle knew it.

"No day is good right now, is it, John." She said it anyway.

"It's getting better." I tried my best to fill my empty eyes with a shade of optimism.

Michelle stepped out of the house and shut the door behind her. "John. We love our grand-daughter. You know that. She is everything to us, and we want to help you. But we cannot, we just simply cannot shuttle her back and forth like this. She needs a schedule."

"I know—"

"Listen, John. You know how much we want to help you and Lou. We plan on being there for both of you today, tomorrow, and whenever you need us. But we—no, *she*—needs a routine to count on. Normalcy, John. She must know you want to be there for the things that matter. Don't you want to be there for the things that matter?"

"Well *of course* I do."

She looked at her watch. "Today Bob's got clients all day. He's not an option. So I can keep her until two—two-thirty at the very latest and then I have appointments of my own."

"Thank you—"

"But I cannot do the conference at school, John.

It's at three-fifteen. Take her with you. She can sit in the library."

"Okay." I looked at my watch for absolutely no reason at all.

She reached up and took my hand while I was still pretending to care what time it was. "John, you must not check out today. She needs you to be there for her. We all need you to be there for her."

I smiled so weakly it might not have looked like a smile at all.

"Come to dinner tonight, would you, please? Bob and I want to discuss some things."

I always suspected Bob and Michelle didn't think much of my intelligence. That moment was another reminder.

"We'll see."

Her expression was not a confident one. I'd seen it on her husband's face many times since I stood on that same porch a day after Emma Jane's sixteenth birthday.

"Two-thirty then. Maybe take her to the park or something before. She'd like that."

"Alright." But my mind was already gone, back at the side of Route 11 where in-laws weren't welcome and time was relative.

Nineteen
The Interview

I hadn't meant to visit them that day.

Before I knew Lou Lou was out of school, I had good intentions for that Tuesday in early October. I had written a to-do list on the back of a Chinese food menu the night before. Visiting the crosses wasn't on it.

The harvest was ending and some of the men hadn't been paid in three weeks.

Scott was planning to visit later in the week and the house needed to be cleaned. Badly.

The grass around the three crosses on the orchard needed to be cut one more time before winter.

Not surprisingly, the insurance company had deemed the van a total loss. At least that's what our insurance agent in Woodstock said in his four voicemail messages. A simple phone call back to him would send the van from a repair shop in Strasburg to the junkyard. A call I wasn't ready to make.

Perhaps the toughest chore that awaited me was disposing of the baby clothes, diapers, wipes, and pacifiers Emma Jane had bought in advance of Baby Willard's arrival. The pile sat on the floor of what should have been the nursery. I hadn't done anything but briefly look inside and shut the door again. But I knew Scott would encourage me to get it done. So would my in-laws, if they knew I hadn't yet.

You've had a tough morning, I told myself as I cruised down Route 11. *You owe it to yourself.*

I'd become at ease with the flashbacks that flooded me each time the site came into view. More than at ease.

I arrived at the clearing, the crosses, the tree line in the distance that continued to eat what was left of the rotting deer. The man with the hobby was back. This time he wore dark green gardening gloves that looked too big for his hands.

Him again, I thought. Scanning the road north and south I again saw no vehicles, no one waiting.

He was on his knees with his back to the road, pulling weeds from the base of Willard's cross.

"You're back," I began.

"So are you." He did not turn around.

I took a long, slow path around the crosses and faced him. "I told you I appreciate this, but it's not necessary."

He held up a piece of Broomsedge. "Have you ever noticed how small weeds can be?"

"Excuse me?"

"Not impressive, is it?" He pulled more weeds and tossed them to the side. "It's a pasture weed."

"And."

He stood up and removed his gloves. His gaze went back down to the crosses, and he appeared to admire his work. "You weren't here earlier, but this looks nicer. Much nicer."

I rubbed and pulled at my left earlobe. "Well, thank you. But you didn't need to come back."

He made eye contact with me for the first time that morning. "Would you give a stranger a ride?"

"I'm sorry?"

"A ride. Would you give me a ride?"

"Where?"

"New Market."

"New Market?"

He smiled. "New Market, Virginia. Founded by General John Sevier, established formally by charter in 1796. Located south on—"

"I know where New Market is."

"Shall we go then?"

I watched him turn and walk back to the shoulder of the road. He looked both ways, either for traffic or to see which direction I'd parked, I don't know which, and began walking toward my truck.

I bent down by Emma Jane's cross. The grass around it was green and trimmed. There wasn't a weed within a ten-foot radius. Willard's cross had drifted slightly to the side and I carefully straightened it, pressing the soil around its base and nudging it in micro movements until it matched his mother's. Perfectly vertical.

There was more I wanted to say to them that day, but "I miss you" was all that came out of my mouth before I made my way back to the road. I walked to my truck and was relieved to see him leaning against the passenger door. At that point I wouldn't have been surprised if the odd man had hot-wired and stolen it.

"New Market?" I asked again as I approached and pressed the unlock button on my key ring.

He answered with two thumbs-up and was in the truck with his seat belt on by the time I opened my own door and climbed in.

"What's in New Market?"

"Another site."

"Site?"

"Memorial."

I turned the key and put the truck in reverse. "You're serious about this."

"About what?"

"These memorials. Crash sites."

"You didn't believe me?"

"I guess I did, yes." I began backing the truck onto Route 11. "Which way. Interstate or 11?"

"How about we go the long way?"

The long way.

I pulled onto Route 11 headed south. "I don't really have time for this." I thought I'd mumbled the words loud enough for him to hear, but not necessarily clearly enough to understand.

"Busy day?"

I adjusted my mirror and we rode without speaking until passing through Maurertown.

"You know the Shenandoah Valley pretty well?" he asked just as a white MINI Cooper blazed past us when the road widened to two lanes.

"Idiot . . . Not you," I clarified.

"I knew what you meant."

"Yes. I know the area."

He looked out the passenger's window. "It's gorgeous here. A slice of heaven, don't you think?"

"I guess."

We passed the WELCOME TO WOODSTOCK sign.

"You mind answering a question?" he said.

"You mind asking it first?"

"A wise request. I'm always curious . . . How long ago did you suffer your loss?"

I knew the exact number of days since they'd been killed on August 23rd, but such an answer wouldn't support my ongoing efforts to appear— stable. "A month, month and a half, I guess. Why?"

"Like I said. Always curious."

We sat at the light at Main and Court streets, the center of Woodstock. A group of young children walked across Main in front of us with chaperones at the front, back, and middle. They herded them safely from our left to our right and began walking up Court Street toward the firehouse. I wondered if they were students at the preschool in the basement of the Presbyterian Church. More important, *are they on a field trip to the firehouse?*

I sensed my passenger was watching me and I turned my head.

He was.

"It's peaceful, isn't it?"

"What?"

"Children."

"Sure."

"The way they trust. The way they learn by watching."

"I guess."

The light turned green and we continued south through downtown.

"You have children?" he asked.

"Uh-huh."

"How many?"

I'd not been asked this question since the accident. I took a moment. "Just one."

"The one who passed?"

"No, a daughter. She's five."

"Oh. So you have two children."

"I guess I do, yes."

He didn't press further so I offered, "I have a daughter. She's in kindergarten."

"What's her name?"

"Lou Lou. We—*I*—call her Lou Lou."

He smiled. "Lou Lou. That's a sweet name. Lou Lou."

I smiled back at hearing a stranger say it for the first time in a while. "Yes, it is."

"Is she in school today?"

I pressed the gas and sped through the yellow light at the intersection of Routes 11 and 42. A car pulling onto 11 from the Sheetz parking lot on the corner honked at me when I nearly clipped him.

"No, she's not. It's a holiday."

I sensed he wanted to ask another question about her.

He didn't.

"So you know the Valley well."

"As well as last time you asked."

"How long have you lived here?"

"I was born here."

"In Woodstock?"

"No, Strasburg."

"There's not a hospital in Strasburg."

I looked at him. "You're right."

"Hmm. It sounds interesting."

"It's not really."

"Try me."

I began driving faster as we neared the Inn at Narrow Passage and was doing seventy when we breezed past it and toward the north edge of Edinburg.

"You don't need to tell me." He looked away

from me and back out his window. "I'm just enjoying the company."

"My mother was pregnant with me." I tried to recall when I'd last told the story. "She was a single mother. Young. Made some dumb choices, obviously. She lived in the city but was out here in the Valley for some reason and had a crash."

"I'm sorry."

"Doesn't matter. I never met her. I was born. She died. I was adopted."

"And here you are."

"Uh-huh."

Edinburg was already behind us. The road flattened as we drove on to Mount Jackson. I passed a VDOT tractor mowing the waist-high grass on the right side of the road.

"Do you know much about her?"

"Who."

"Your birth mother."

"Only what a stack of papers tells me."

A mile later we passed a cross on the side of the road I'd never noticed before. It had a half-deflated balloon tied to it. He watched it closely as we passed. "Good people," he whispered.

"Sorry?"

"I said 'good people.' That family."

"You know them?"

"Not well," he said but quickly added, "well enough."

We navigated the small town of Mount Jackson,

and I again picked up speed as we cleared the business district and rolled by industrial buildings and, later, farmland. The leaves on the mountains to the east were changing, and for a mile or two I allowed myself to remember how much I loved the fall. The colors, the wind, the crisp but comfortable evenings. I missed how much Emma Jane loved the fall, too.

My quiet passenger creased the silence. "Would you mind a quick detour?"

Evidently I didn't answer soon enough.

"It will only take a moment. Turn right up at Meem's."

"Meem's Bottom? The covered bridge? What the heck for?"

"It will only take a moment."

I began to wish for the first time since the first visit to the crosses that I'd stayed home that day. "Why not." I turned right on Wissler by the corn maze and pulled off the road to the left in a small gravel lot just shy of the bridge.

"It will only take a moment," he said as he got out of the truck.

"Yeah, you said that," I muttered just after his door shut.

The man walked across the bridge, stopping for a few minutes about halfway across before completing the span and stopping again on the far side. He stood on a short rock wall at the edge overlooking the shallow river below.

I stepped out of the truck and walked to the head of the trail on my side of the bridge that took visitors down a slope to the river's edge. From where I stood, the strange man appeared motionless on his side of the river and bridge for almost five minutes.

The bridge was hardly new to me. I'd been there many times through my years in the Valley and had pictures of Emma Jane and Lou Lou standing on the bridge just a year earlier when we came with another couple and their two children to experience the maze. We spent ninety minutes laughing and running, getting very lost in the vast cornfield carved into trails of adventure.

I began to cross the bridge and called to him in stride. "You coming?"

He did not acknowledge me.

"Are you alright?" I stepped more slowly the closer I got.

Only when I was so close I could have touched him did he turn to me. "I'm fine."

I looked around for a memorial. Nothing. No cross. No marker. Just me and the man who called himself the Cross Gardener standing on a twelve-inch-wide rock wall that fell off to a river.

He remained so deep in thought, so lost, I wasn't sure he'd even hear me ask. But my gut said he wanted me to. "So what's the deal here."

"Deal?" His eyes were focused down on the river.

"This place. The bridge. Is this one of yours?"

He swiveled his head. "No, no. This isn't one of mine. None of the places are mine." He stepped off the wall to the surface of the road. "I just tend to them."

"Alright. Well listen, I don't exactly know what you need from me, but if you want your lift to New Market, we need to get moving. I've got to be back soon."

I looked at my watch. Somehow it was approaching noon already.

"I think I'll skip the New Market site today."

A question I would have swallowed back in if I could have: "Because?"

He looked around him, turning in a complete 360-degree circle. "Someone's coming soon. And this place needs attention. You understand."

I looked again for a cross or grave marker of some kind.

"You wonder if someone died here."

He took my silence as a yes.

"A long time ago."

"But there's no cross. There's no memorial."

He nodded. "That's true." Then he looked across the bridge toward Route 11. "But not all suffering has a cross, does it?"

This time he must have taken my silence as a no. In both cases he'd been right.

"I've been told that soon a couple from Montana will visit here, grandparents of a young man who took his life on this bridge many years ago. They've never been here, but today they fulfill a promise to pay their respects in person."

I was captured by the light in his eyes.

"Sometimes in my work I think I forget that suffering happens everywhere, even when there is no cross. Or, perhaps, the cross is there. We just don't see it."

I dug my hands in the pockets of my dirty jeans for the second anxious time that day.

On the other side of the bridge an older couple parked a white Cadillac and trudged up the hill to the entrance of the bridge. The woman walked with a cane. The man held open a map and though we couldn't yet hear them, the two were talking back and forth.

"You can go, John. I'm sorry to have kept you."

I raised my hand and waved off his apology. "It's nothing."

He looked at me a final time that day. "No, it was something. Thank you for the ride. Thank you for the time."

"How will you get to New Market?"

"Not to worry about today. I'll get there. Soon, I'm sure."

I looked around a final time and appreciated the beauty of the bridge and the scene I was a player in. When I looked back to him he'd already walked away to meet the couple. I passed them on my way back to the truck and the man and woman offered hellos. My passenger winked a good-bye but did not smile.

From inside the truck I watched awhile as the couple studied a map closely and examined the bridge. After a few moments apart, the woman stepped toward the side of the bridge and leaned into it, her hands on the wooden beams. The man, her husband I assumed, came to her side and embraced the frail woman.

My passenger remained at a distance from the curious couple.

A very odd witness.

A strange Cross Gardener.

I did not take the long way back to my own site on Route 11 halfway between Strasburg and Toms Brook. I took 81 and I sped.

Lying on my back was comfortable. The ground was secure. Steadying. It was balanced. I was close enough to Baby Willard's cross that with my right hand I could hold its base like a little hand at the exact point it entered the ground.

When I woke up the sky said rain was coming.

My watch said it was 3:10.

Twenty
Stick Figures

I'D had my heart broken before.

The day Tim died in the ocean on a senior trip in Maryland.

The first time Emma Jane said *no* to me.

The night over dinner when Father told us he was dying of lung cancer.

The moment I looked through the small square window in Lou Lou's classroom door and saw my mother-in-law and daughter sitting side by side across from Ms. Silvious. Lou Lou was holding Shell and listening.

Michelle was smiling and turning toward Lou Lou every now and then, patting her knee or stroking the back of her hair.

Ms. Silvious had a manila folder open in front of her with a stack of drawings and worksheets. She looked up and saw me. "Come in," her lips mouthed and she beckoned with her hand.

I walked in and pulled a small chair up next to Lou Lou.

"We're so glad you could make it," said Ms. Silvious.

I'd forgotten how smooth her Valley accent was. Just smooth enough to remind me she was from the South. But not distracting. Just like Emma Jane.

"I'm sorry I'm a little late." I braced for whatever Michelle had to say, no doubt something well deserved.

She looked at me and smiled. "It's okay, John. We're just glad you're here."

Ms. Silvious resumed showing off Lou Lou's alphabet worksheets and drawings. She praised Lou Lou's work and reading level. "She's at least one grade level ahead of most students in the class. She loves her books."

Lou Lou beamed.

I bent down and asked Shell how he was doing. "You have fun at Grandma's?" I whispered.

Shell raised his right hand.

"Good. Sorry I'm late, big guy. Forgive me?"

Shell raised his right hand again.

I draped my arm around Lou Lou and pulled her into my side.

She rested her head against my chest.

"Any questions?" Ms. Silvious asked as she closed Lou Lou's file.

Michelle looked at me, deferring.

"It looks like she's doing great, right?" I said with enthusiasm.

"She's doing fine, yes, Mr. Bevan."

"Super." I looked at Michelle. "Questions?"

She shook her head.

"Let's get out of the way then and keep you on

schedule." I rose and shook Ms. Silvious's hand. "Sorry again about being late. I was tied up."

"Apology accepted." She shook hands with both Lou Lou and Michelle. "See you tomorrow, Lou Lou?"

Lou Lou nodded.

"I can't wait," Ms. Silvious added. "Would you and your grandmother mind waiting outside for your dad? I want to talk to him for just one more minute. Alright?"

"Come on, sweetheart." Michelle took Lou Lou's hand and led her into the hallway. She shut the door behind her.

"Uh-oh," I said, taking my seat again. "How bad is it? Cigarettes? Boys?" I laughed the only way that seemed natural anymore. Nervously.

Ms. Silvious pulled a drawing from the bottom of the stack and held it up. "I thought you should see this."

She held the white sheet of paper by the top corners. A stick figure drawn in brown crayon knelt by a black cross. Beneath it a flat line of green grass ran from one edge of the paper to the other. Simple trees, fat vertical lines with X's at the top, filled the background. A second, much smaller cross was drawn two inches away from the first. A big round yellow sun filled the upper right corner of the paper; a gray cloud filled the left.

I wanted to say something before Ms. Silvious did. But I didn't know what.

"This concerns me," she began and handed the picture to me.

I studied it more closely.

"This is the cemetery, I presume, where Mrs. Bevan and your son are buried."

"No," I said and shook my head. "It's not."

"I'm sorry then, I just assumed."

"It's the place where the accident happened."

"I see."

"That's her, right?" I pointed at the stick figure.

"No, that's probably you."

"Did she say that?"

"No, but that's not how she would draw herself, Mr. Bevan."

"Please call me John."

"Alright." She smiled. "Then I'm Kerri." She flipped through the drawings and set aside three. Then she held each up. "See here"—she gestured—"when Lou draws herself, even as a stick figure, she puts curls in her hair. That's typical, in fact, of most children. They draw girls or mothers with curls and boys or men without hair at all." She showed another drawing of two figures, one tall and skinny, the other short with curly hair. They were holding hands by a misshapen tree with four fat green apples. "This is you." She pointed again.

"I got that."

She again closed the folder and pushed it to the side. "I don't mean to pry, that's not my job, but

I am concerned about her. I know Mrs. Payne, the counselor, is also. And, incidentally, she apologizes that she couldn't be here for this."

I stood up and walked to a bulletin board of finger paintings.

Ms. Silvious paused, then followed and stood beside me.

"John, the turtle—"

"Shell."

"Yes, Shell, he's a coping mechanism. Have you heard that term before?"

"Of course."

"It's a comfort, a companion, and it's not uncommon given how recent this loss—this tragic loss—was for you both. But it's less common for this companion, a blanket if you will, to do all the talking for her." She took a few steps sideways and away from me.

I wondered what scent bothered her most. The skipped shower, the bridge, the afternoon asleep at the crosses, or the grief.

"Don't you think the thing with the turtle will pass?"

"It should. But how long will it take? Every day she waits to begin expressing herself again is another step away, and eventually she'll have to take those steps back to you. It's important that you're not moving in the opposite direction either."

I found the desk with her name stenciled on construction paper at the top.

This time Ms. Silvious—Kerri—did not follow me. "John, I am out of my comfort zone diagnosing a child. As I said, this isn't my job. Not at all. But I do think from what I see each day, just from my point of view, she needs to be seeing someone who does have this expertise."

I sat at Lou Lou's desk in a tiny tan plastic chair with metal legs.

"Do you agree?" she asked, still standing across the room. Arms folded.

A book in Lou Lou's desk about bunnies made me smile. "I don't know."

Her voice softened and, without looking over, I sensed she was moving toward me. "There is no one in Lou Lou's life, or your life, that doesn't feel such sorrow for what you've experienced. I didn't know your wife well, but many here at Sandy Hook did, and I've heard her dream was to teach here eventually."

"It was."

"Then please understand just how much everyone wants to support your family right now. One way we do that is by watching Lou Lou closely, so very closely. This time in her healing is the most critical."

For a woman who's not trained to treat children, you sure do a lot of it. I was thankful I'd thought the words before giving them life. "You're right," I said. "But she's going to be fine. She just needs me and the orchard. And some time."

"Absolutely. And you just keep loving her, more than ever, and if you don't think she needs more help right now, we'll support that . . . For now . . . And we'll all pray she begins to open up again."

"Agreed."

The young teacher now stood in front of me. She placed her hand on my arm. "She's a gem, John, such a bright, kind girl. You should be very proud." She handed me a piece of paper with her personal contact information on it. "If you have any concerns at all, please don't hesitate to contact me. Here are my numbers and e-mail address."

I thanked her, tucked the paper in my back pocket, apologized again for being late, and said good-bye. I left the classroom and found Lou Lou and Michelle reading books in the library.

"I'm sorry, Michelle."

She took Lou Lou's hand and led her to me. "You and Lou Lou coming for dinner?"

I lifted Lou Lou off the ground and she wrapped her legs around my waist. "I'd love to."

That's what stick figures do sometimes. They lie.

Twenty-one
Pork Chops

It was probably the best pork chop I'd ever eaten.

Maybe it had been too long since I'd had one. Or maybe it had just been too long since I'd had a meal not served in a bucket, bag, or box. The accompanying green peas in cream, salad, and rolls were just as tasty. Even comforting. Lou Lou and I both devoured the meal without much more than an occasional grunt.

Dessert was vanilla bean ice cream with chocolate sauce for Lou Lou and caramel for me. It hadn't been nearly as long since we'd had ice cream. In fact, the freezer was full of the same brand.

Bob and Michelle made small talk throughout dinner. After Lou Lou knocked her ice-cream spoon to the floor, Bob began a story I'd never heard about Emma Jane in a Golden Corral on her twelfth birthday dropping a bowl of ice cream on her favorite Sunday shoes.

"I'd have cried right on the spot," Michelle said, taking over. "But that girl just looked down, took a deep breath, and laughed. She thought it was the funniest thing. You could hear her across the restaurant. She kicked them right off, held them over the trash by the entrance while the goop dripped off, and walked in her stockings back to our booth at the back of the restaurant. She set them on the floor by her and said—Do you remember what she said, Bob?"

"I sure do."

"She said, 'Well that's what I get for eating out on the Sabbath. The Lord doesn't approve.' "

"Huh?" I said.

"She didn't cry or fuss or argue. She was laughing at herself because she always thought we were breaking a commandment by eating out on Sunday, but was waiting for a sign. And there it was."

"A sign right on her favorite shoes," Bob added.

Michelle looked at Lou Lou. "Your grandpa and I still had dinner out on Sunday now and then, but she never joined us after that. She took a stand."

Lou Lou looked up at me, waiting, perhaps, for me to be polite. "That's a nice story. She'd never told it. Just said that she didn't feel right eating out or shopping on Sunday. And we never did."

"I'd be stunned to hear otherwise," Bob said, and he excused himself to clear the ice-cream bowls. "That was our Emma Jane."

Our Emma Jane, I thought, and if the pork chop hadn't been so good I might have corrected him out loud.

The rest of us made our way into the living room, and Michelle sat on the love seat. Lou Lou and I walked on by to the front door and were slipping on our shoes when Bob stopped me from the doorway to the kitchen. "Do you have another minute?"

I didn't. But the pork chop and much-too-easily-forgiven nap on the side of Route 11 said I'd better. "Sure."

"Lou Lou, there are some new books upstairs on your bed. Would you like to go up and read them for a little while?"

Lou Lou looked at me for approval, which I enjoyed giving in their presence, and she and Shell raced up the stairs. Bunny was there, too, her head poking out of Shell's backpack and bobbing up and down with each step.

Bob motioned to a black leather reading chair. "Sit a minute, if you would."

I did, and I could have finished their first sentences for them.

"John, Bob and I have been talking a lot lately about Lou Lou."

I bet you have.

"We don't need to tell you how much we love her."

"No, you don't. She loves you, too."

"That's right," Bob said. "She does. And every day we spend with her she seems to open up more."

"Open up? You're having real conversations with her? Back and forth?"

"Well no." Bob shifted. "Not yet—"

"So she's opening up how?"

"Now, John," Michelle said, "this isn't a debate . . ."

Exactly.

"We don't want to make you feel defensive . . ."

Then don't try.

"We just want what's best for our grand-daughter."

"Me, too. I work on that every day."

"Do you?" Bob said.

I quickly took to my feet. "Okay, let's get this done. I haven't showered today, which you must have noticed, and it's been a long day for my daughter. Why are we here? You want Lou Lou to stay for a couple nights?"

Bob and Michelle exchanged a glance. He gave her knee a squeeze and she stood. "We were thinking longer."

I rubbed my left earlobe before crossing my arms. "How long?"

Michelle took two steps toward me. "For as long as it takes, sweetheart."

"As long as it takes for what? Do you have any idea how much more difficult you've made this by not just saying whatever it is you've rehearsed? Get it out or we're walking out the door."

"Bob . . ." She looked over her shoulder and he joined her side, even wrapping his arm around

153

her in an embarrassing attempt at a unified front.

"We want her to stay indefinitely, John. A couple weeks, maybe a month, maybe until the holidays if that's how long it takes for her to begin recovering. And, quite frankly, for you to begin healing as well."

It was even worse than I'd expected. This was premeditated, and probably on their schedule whether I'd been late that day or not. *Emma Jane would never have done this,* I thought. "You two are quite an act." I moved to the stairs and took two before she begged me to stop.

"What, Michelle, you want me to just hand my child to you? Give you all I have left? Because she's not *talking* enough?"

"She's not talking at all, John, she's completely withdrawn. We can help her."

"And so can I." I said the words with my back to them as I ascended the stairs and opened the door to the room they'd designated as hers since her first visit post-accident. Lou Lou had fallen asleep. Shell was under her head. Bunny was in her arms. The moment stopped. Not because of some otherworldly slow-motion special effect, but because I could not look away.

Watching a child sleep from a partially open door in the calming light of fall dusk is something best done with a woman at your side.

Sometime later, I don't know quite how long, I walked back down the stairs and found Bob and

Michelle pacing nervously—and so pre-
dictably—in the living room.

"She can stay the night. I'll come for her
tomorrow." I walked out the door and down the
walk toward my truck.

Once again Bob's voice stopped me. "Son, we
only want to help you both."

"I'm not your son. And if you want to help, let
me be her father."

If I had been Bob, I would have fired back with
something snappy like, *Then be her father.*

But the diplomatic accountant simply nodded
his head.

From the step-up to the truck I called out a final
jab. "Emma Jane would have never tried something like this."

Bob volleyed back with a retort I couldn't
answer. "Maybe not, but she wouldn't be sulking
away her days on the side of the road either."

So much for diplomatic.

Twenty-two
No One Dies Alone

I didn't sleep a second that night.

I rolled over to Emma Jane's side of the bed
and back again. I walked to Lou Lou's empty
room and lay on her Barbie-themed bed, feet

hanging off the bottom. I counted the glow-in-the-dark stars on her ceiling. Emma Jane made me so angry putting those up when she was already four months pregnant with Willard. I came home to see her on a stepstool attempting to stick them up in the pattern of the Big Dipper with Lou Lou on the bed below directing her with a laser pointer.

I couldn't stay angry long. Now I wish I hadn't gotten angry at all. The stars looked beautiful, though nothing like the Big Dipper, and reminded me that the bed in my room was empty.

I sat on the floor in the nursery that wasn't a nursery. Lou Lou's crib had come out of storage and was disassembled, leaning against the wall in five pieces. I cleared a space in the middle of the room and put it together, just to see if I could without help. I did. But before shutting the door I made a note to return and take it down again before anyone saw.

Then, like so many mornings, I sat on the couch and ate a bowl of cold cereal. Then a second. I turned on the TV and wished Lou Lou and Shell were sitting next to me. Billy Mays was selling widgets and cleaners on three different channels, and it looked as if Senator Barack Obama was selling change on all the others. I personally wasn't a junkie, but Emma Jane had sure loved politics. The horse race. The debates. The issues. The passion. We buried her twenty-four hours before Governor Sarah Palin was selected as Senator John McCain's running mate and I would have given anything to hear Emma Jane's opinion.

Without her to provide commentary throughout the election season, the entire race seemed pointless. Annoying commercials. Nasty sound bites. I had enough wrong in my life without needing to be reminded the country was headed off a cliff no matter who we elected. I wasn't even sure I'd vote anymore.

I turned the TV off and pulled a pair of jeans and a flannel shirt from the dryer. I didn't think there should have been a difference in how they smelled. But there was. Nothing smelled the same since Emma Jane had died.

Yesterday was a difficult day, I reminded myself and considered leaving right then to pick up Lou Lou from my in-laws. That's what they'd expect, I decided.

Instead I did what felt most natural. I went to the crosses.

The sun was still rising when I pulled off the orchard, but already the man who'd offered to handle my accounts was on the property talking midway down a row to a group of pickers. I'd not had the courage to do my Apple Math yet and run estimates on what I'd earned, but I knew it wouldn't be good news. My meager profits, if there were any left, would be split that year, and Lou Lou and I faced a long recovery.

Still, I couldn't wait for the harvest to be done and the orchard cleared of Spanish speakers and apple bins.

The drive to the crosses was so familiar I arrived without remembering much of the trip. *Would the stranger be there?* I parked in my usual spot off the road and began the walk to the site. A car honked and someone in the passenger seat waved as it passed. I didn't recognize the woman, but she smiled with her mouth closed when our eyes met briefly at forty miles per hour.

He was back. But this time there was no paint, no weeding, just the man called Cross Gardener sitting with his back to the road to the right of the crosses. Not wanting to startle him, I made more noise than I needed to as I approached. But if he heard me coming, he chose not to show it.

"I was hoping you'd come today," he said when I arrived at his side.

"Why's that?" I took a seat on the grass a few steps away and faced him.

"I was hoping for your help."

I looked around. Still no paint, gloves, sandpaper to be seen. "Help with?"

"Another site."

"Didn't I give you a ride just yesterday?"

"That you did. And I was grateful for it. As was the couple on the bridge, I promise you."

"You're welcome." I stared at Emma Jane's and

Baby Willard's crosses. Fresh, peaceful. "I don't know, today's not great, I'm afraid."

"Afraid of what?"

"You know what I mean, afraid today isn't a good day to run around. I'm afraid I need to be here with them today."

"Afraid."

"Was that a question?" I asked.

"No."

We sat quietly a minute.

"I can walk then. You enjoy." He stood and walked toward the road. He did not look back; he did not say good-bye.

Is he waiting for me to stop him? I thought. *Because I won't. Not today.*

I looked back at the crosses and noticed how perfectly straight they were, as if someone had placed a level on them and adjusted by the millimeter until they stood precisely true.

Which way did he go? I looked out to the road and a county sheriff's cruiser rolled past. *He's waiting for me around the corner,* I thought. *So sure I'll come drive him to whatever strange place awaits.*

My bare wrist reminded me I'd forgotten to put my watch on that morning. *Sad how the simple acts become such chores.* There was a growing list of things I'd forgotten lately. Some because people expected me to, others because I could, still others because grief pushed them from their place in line.

My mind returned to the Cross Gardener. *How long would he wait out of view before giving up and walking on?* I stood up, stretched like I'd been sitting for hours, looked to the tree line, rubbed the spot on my wrist where my watch should have been, and stepped to the road.

He was almost out of sight to the north. *He hadn't waited at all.* I jogged to the truck and caught up to him. I rolled down the passenger's-side window. "Climb in, I have a few minutes."

When I stopped, he climbed in but did not speak.

"You knew I'd come, didn't you?"

"No."

"Really?"

"I hoped you would," he said, looking straight ahead. "But I didn't know."

"Uh-huh."

We drove through downtown Strasburg. "So where am I taking you? And how long do you need?"

"Taking *us*." He corrected. "How much time do you have for us?"

I glanced at my wrist, snickered, then looked at the digital clock on the dashboard. "I need to pick up my daughter soon. Probably should have already, really."

"Do you need to make a call?" he offered. "Or perhaps she could come along."

Sitting at the light at 11 in front of the Antique

160

Emporium, we were only a few minutes from Bob and Michelle's. "I'll check. You mind a pit stop?"

"Not at all."

We drove a mile, slightly more, to their home just outside the town limits. "This is the smart move," I said to him—and myself—as I climbed out of the truck in front of their home.

Michelle answered the door.

"Good morning," I forced out believably.

"She's out in the back with Bob. One minute—"

"Wait, Michelle, I just wanted to check on her. I've got a friend in the truck"—I pointed—"who needs a lift real quick. A favor. She could come, but I thought she might like to stay."

Michelle nodded exactly the way I'd predicted. "Of course, John."

"I won't be long."

"Of course."

"This is alright?"

"Go, your friend is waiting."

"After last night I just wanted to be sure—"

"Go on. She'll be fine here another few hours." She looked like she wanted to pull me into a hug. In fact, everything about her body language said she needed, wanted to comfort me. But just because she didn't feel lingering anger from the night before didn't mean I couldn't.

I hid it well. "Thanks, Michelle. I owe you."

"Be safe."

I felt her watching me as I made my way down their sidewalk to the truck.

"Everything alright?" The man asked.

"Too much so."

He must have wanted to ask why, and maybe I wanted to tell him why, but I didn't. We rode back to 11 and toward the freeway. "Where do you need to go?"

"Take 55 headed to West Virginia. You know that area?"

"Of course. I live out there."

Ten minutes later we passed Lebanon Church and I pointed right to Middle Road in the direction of the orchard. "It's down there a few hundred yards. Grew up there and now it's mine."

"Must be nice."

"What?"

"To own an orchard."

"It's work."

"I can only imagine."

We passed into West Virginia and I recalled the last time I'd been that far west on 55. It was in a delivery truck with Emma Jane at my side.

"This is one of my favorite areas," my passenger said.

"It's pretty out here. We have accounts this direction. At least I hope we still do."

He nodded and we raced at eighty miles an hour along a freshly completed stretch of beautiful, wide highway. After we passed Wardensville, he asked me to take the next opportunity to exit and get on Old Route 55. The winding two-lane road was the only 55 Father and many of the earlier workers on the orchard ever knew.

But I knew the road well, and I knew the two crosses in the trees on the right side of the road even better.

"Pull over here."

"What is this?"

"A memorial, of course." His tone had a slight snap.

I stopped the truck just before a bridge and he got out before I'd even put it in park. He reached into the truck bed and pulled out a can of paint with two brushes and two pairs of gloves resting on the lid. With his other hand he retrieved a machete.

I jumped out my side of the truck. "Where did those—"

"Hope you don't mind."

"When did—"

"Back at the other site. Like I said, I hoped you'd come."

He set down the paint can and the brushes, tossed a pair of gloves to me, put on the other, and took the machete into the trees. In careful swipes he sliced through seasons of thick green brush and weeds. "Could you clear this out?"

"Sure." *Am I really standing on the side of the road clearing brush at crosses my father planted twenty years ago?* I'd had a lot of strange, unexplainable dreams since Emma Jane and the baby died, but none quite as odd as this.

Brush and branches were piling up at my feet. "Can you get those?" he asked again and continued clearing out a wide circle around the crosses, still dwarfed by years of inattention. He was so precise, strong but delicate, taking great care to cut only what needed to be cut.

Finally I remembered the gloves I was holding, put them on, and threw an armful of brush into the back of the truck.

"There you go," I think he said from his spot in the trees.

Mostly I just watched and waited for another pile of junk to gather up and toss in the truck. It was amazing, at least to me, how much he was able to clear. It must have taken a half hour for him to trim the area well enough that from the side of the road both crosses were easily visible from all angles. Without being asked, I thought to cross the street and check the view from straight on, then fifty or sixty yards in one direction, and the same distance in the other.

When I got back to the crosses he was on his knees stirring the paint with a stick.

"Grab a brush," he said.

I did, and I knelt next to him.

"That was a lot of growth," he said, still stirring.

"Years' worth," I said, because I knew.

"I think you're right . . . Before you take your gloves off, could you wipe down both crosses?"

With my hands I swept away spiderwebs and dirt. Bird droppings. Dead bugs and a few live ones. "Sandpaper would be better."

"Indeed . . ." And he produced a piece, I thought, from his back pocket. "Here you go."

He continued stirring and I gently sanded away the imperfections of time.

"That's good enough," he said.

"It's not perfect."

"It never is. But it's close enough." He tapped the stick on the side of the paint can before resting it on a rock. He stuck his brush in the paint, also tapped it to remove the excess, and handed it to me. "Switch."

We exchanged brushes and I began painting the cross nearest me. The wood was rotting near the bottom, but the rest was surprisingly strong. There was barely enough color left from the first time it was painted to know it was once bright white.

"How did you know?" I asked and dipped my brush for another coat.

"Know what?"

"Come on. How did you know about this place? Why did you bring me here?"

"I'm the Cross Gardener. I know where a lot of memorials are."

I finally looked at him. *Come on,* my face must have said.

"When's the last time you were here?" he asked.

"To pay respects? A long time. But I've driven by."

"Do you say a quick and simple prayer when you just drive by without stopping?"

Not really, I thought.

"Well you should. They appreciate it."

I didn't ask.

He sanded away on the other cross.

"So you knew about these men?"

"I'd heard."

"Heard what?"

"That they worked for your father."

The cross I painted was clean and white. Pure again. I set my brush on the paint lid and stood up. "So why did you bring me here?"

He remained kneeling and began to paint his own. "Why do *you* think I brought you here?"

"If I knew I wouldn't—"

"Have asked?"

"That's right." I took a few steps back and couldn't avoid admiring my work. "What you're doing, it's good work. I get it. But why me and why here? These crosses are all but forgotten."

He dipped his brush in the paint for a second coat. "Not forgotten."

"Maybe, but neglected, obviously."

166

He reached behind the cross to paint the side no one would ever see unless they traipsed through the woods. "Perhaps their loved ones grieved elsewhere."

"Maybe."

"Perhaps not all suffering has a cross, John. And not all crosses have suffering."

How so? I thought.

"In my work, this special mission of mine, I see people overlook suffering because there is no cross."

"And?"

"And it's a mistake. Sometimes you can't *see* the cross, John. People all around us are suffering, struggling with depression, addiction, stress, loss of faith. But unless they are carrying a cross or holding some other sign, we walk past them."

"So not all suffering has a cross," I said. "I get it, I guess."

I watched him quietly paint for another moment or two. When he was finished he also stood and stepped back to appreciate his work.

"Did *you* know them, too?" I asked.

"Not personally."

"But you knew they were friends of my family?"

"Friends or workers?" he asked.

"Both. I was a child. But they were certainly friends of my father. He planted these crosses. *We* planted them. I remember my father arranged for their bodies to be shipped to Mexico."

"I know."

It was the opening I'd waited for. "What else do you know about us?"

He stepped back to the paint and bent over to put the lid back on.

"Well?" I pressed.

He put the paint and brushes back in the bed of the truck. "I know you're suffering like the wives of these two men did."

"How do you know that?"

"How could I not? They lost their sweethearts in this spot and they've probably never been able to travel here and spend time. They must have been devastated. Think of it." He stared back to the crosses, standing so much straighter now, proud. "They probably wondered how it happened and never knew with certainty." He retrieved the gloves and machete from the ground and also placed them in the truck. "All those tears the wives and their children must have shed. So much sadness thinking their husbands died alone on a dark highway."

"That's how it goes," I said, putting one foot on the running board and resting my arms on top of the bed liner. "Some loved ones die in hospital beds, some die at home. Some die alone on the side of the road."

He mimicked me, awkwardly I thought, on his side of the truck.

"You're right. Some do pass through in hospitals, or in the sweet comfort of their living rooms, some even at places like this." He gestured with both hands at the ground around us. "But no one dies alone."

Twenty-three
Resistance

NO one dies alone.
The Cross Gardener's words stayed with me that night when I tucked Lou Lou into bed. They stayed with me when I sat on the porch and listened to cars whiz and flash down 55 at the bottom of the driveway. They ran through my mind again as I walked by bright starlight to the highest point of the orchard where Grandpa's, Tim's, and Father's graves were marked by fading and chipped wooden crosses.

The Shenandoah Valley's October air was finally thinning. Indian summer humidity and annual allergies were replaced with comfortable, comforting air you couldn't wait to breathe when the sun set at the end of a long, exhausting harvest day.

Except that I hadn't spent the day harvesting.

I lay down on the grass and weeds and put my hands under my head.

No one dies alone.

When my father died, I was aware enough to capture the list of standard lines mourners feel obligated to share.

"At least he's not in pain."

"Your dad was such a great man."

"Wayne Bevan lived such a good life."

"He was so proud of you."

"Wayne's free now."

When Emma Jane died, the cloud around me absorbed most of the platitudes and I don't remember being comforted by any of the rote condolences. I was going to mourn the way I deserved to mourn. That's the grand prize for a mother, brother, father, and then a perfectly healthy wife in her twenties.

No one dies alone.

Hadn't Tim died alone in the morning surf off Ocean City, Maryland?

It had only been twelve hours since Tim drowned. Father was standing in the lobby of an oceanfront hotel talking to two investigators. The grief-stricken principal stood with them, still shaking, still crying, still apologizing as if she'd personally held his head under the salty water.

Scott and I sat on a couch across the lobby eating a bag of Cheetos. I don't know what Scott was thinking, but I was wondering if anyone could tell I was trying so hard not to cry that my stomach hurt.

Tim had had the world in front of him, literally. He was eighteen. A senior. He wanted to travel the world and lead hunting trips to exotic foreign places like Africa and Wyoming. He was out in the ocean with nothing between him and the other side of the world he'd never get to see.

I imagined he was on his back, floating happily, dreaming of shotguns and big game. Thinking of the day he'd sleep in a tent with elephants and giraffes wandering around his campsite. Thinking of how much Grandpa Bevan would have loved to be at his side, holding a rifle and tracking dangerous beasts on those foreign adventures.

He drowned. Was it painful? Did he suffer? Did he see his dreams fade as the water covered his face the final time, or did they become more crisp and colorful? Did he see God? Did he see anyone at all?

I overheard the principal say that Tim had ventured out alone early in the morning for a swim without telling anyone. He hadn't been drinking. He wasn't horsing around the way teenagers can.

But he was alone.

Had he become scared? Tired? Did he get swept under? Lose his bearings?

One of the high school guidance counselors and her husband, both chaperones, were walking along the beach at sunrise when they saw something floating in the water.

They stepped into the surf.

They ran to the hotel.

They called the police.

The police called Father.

Father picked us up from school early and told us the news on the journey to Ocean City.

"Boys, your brother has died."

"What?" Scott asked.

"Tim drowned in the ocean this morning, son. We're driving there now."

Scott was so smart; even as a middle schooler it seemed he was always the smartest of the brothers. And he was older than me. Wiser. But still I remember him staring at Father in the front seat of our truck and saying, "I don't understand."

Scott and I stayed and watched TV in a room the hotel arranged for us while Father went to the local hospital to identify Tim and arrange for his body to be transported to Strasburg.

On the way home the next morning Father told us not to be sad and that Tim wouldn't want us to sulk. But not just that, I remember how Father filled all the miles with similar counsel. I figured that's what fathers must do to handle their own sadness.

"He sure loved to swim, didn't he, boys?"

"Perhaps he's finally seeing what Africa looks like."

"He's free now."

At some point Father stopped talking and asked if we had any questions of our own.

Scott asked where Tim would be buried.

I asked why Tim had broken the rules.

Scott asked if Father thought Tim would go to heaven.

I asked how Tim would find it.

Twenty-four
Stranger Funeral

W AS it the first time I was genuinely glad to see him?

I dropped off Lou Lou at school right on time and that put us both in a good mood. She waved at me as one of her shadows looped an arm through hers. I waved back and drove to check on the crosses. Not to spend the day, I pledged in the rearview mirror, but to say hello. Be sure they were standing straight. Unharmed.

Because I didn't think I'd be staying long, I bypassed my usual spot and pulled right into the clearing and onto the grass behind the crosses, safely away from the road. The Cross Gardener was standing there, in a white shirt and tie, like we'd had an appointment and as if there were absolutely no gardening to do.

"You're persistent," I said, stepping out of the truck.

"So are you." He smiled.

"Actually I'm not staying today. I'm just checking in, a quick visit, that's all."

"Perfect." He clasped his hands. "I need a ride."

"Why am I not surprised?"

"You have time?"

That depends, I thought. There was still work to be done at the orchard even though the last of the Braeburns had been picked and the harvest was finished. I no longer had workers to rely on and I was the only one who could handle the orchard's billing. The house was a mess, again, we were out of food, again, both tractors needed repair, and my pickup was due for state inspection before the last day of October.

But in the reality I'd chosen to live, I had plenty of time, and I suspected my new friend knew it.

"I could spare a few hours. Where do you need to go?"

"A funeral in Fort Valley."

"Um. Okay. I'm supposed to wait for you?"

"Yes and no. You drive. I'll explain."

We rode along Route 11 to Edinburg and over the mountain to what locals called the Fort. Though I'd loved our piece of land in Strasburg, I was sure there couldn't be many more beautiful and tranquil places than the Fort.

"You really need a car of your own," I joked as we crested the mountain and began the descent.

"You're not the first to suggest that."

"Still at your mother's?"

"More or less. I'm in a transition state."

"Is that what they call it when you move back home?"

"Actually, I never left. And trust me when I say she likes me around and keeping a close eye. She's one of *those*."

"Then why does it seem like I'm your personal taxi?"

"Because you're a good man."

I'd been joking, but his response was pure.

I apologized with a look.

His grin said it was accepted.

"She sounds like a good woman."

"The best."

We arrived in the Fort and he directed me to a church cemetery near the river. There was a modest crowd assembled around a grave in the far-left corner.

"Someone you know?"

"Yes. Will you come?"

"To the grave? Are you crazy? I'm in jeans, jeans with holes no less."

"No one will care, I promise. We'll stay out of the way."

The Cross Gardener got out of the truck and walked across the church parking lot to the metal gate that led into the cemetery. Then he turned and seemed to be waiting for me.

Seriously? I thought. *I'm not going unless he actually motions for me.*

He did.

"What am I doing?" I muttered. He was smiling, beaming in fact, when I approached him at the gate.

"You knew I'd come, didn't you?"

"No, but I hoped."

We walked in and stood well away from the graveside service. Without an explanation or warning he said, "Wait here," and he stepped closer and closer to the crowd until he was in it.

I didn't know whether to leave him, follow, blend in, or eavesdrop. So I just stood, feeling like a dumb statue, watching complete strangers bury a loved one. I made a mental note to tell my odd friend how uncomfortable he'd left me.

The preacher began to speak, and I quickly learned I wouldn't have to try to eavesdrop at all because he spoke loud enough that I could have heard him from the orchard. "Family and friends, this is a day of celebration, not sadness."

I think I heard a few scattered *amens*.

"Travis would not want us to wail and mourn. That was not his way. He would want us to rejoice and be happy and celebrate his joy for life."

Familiar words.

"Travis was such a loving, kind person with a smile that made you want to smile, too."

I tuned out. They were the boilerplate words I'd heard before from whatever manuals preachers brush off on funeral mornings. I could have given the sermon myself. The truth was that I didn't need to know Travis to know that he was certainly as imperfect as anyone else. *Death's lens is powerful,* I thought.

As the preacher continued I wandered away and around the front half of the cemetery. The markers bore names of soldiers, grandparents, children, and infants. Many of the last names were familiar family names I'd heard growing up in our small county. One man's grave from 2006 had a single white carnation on top. I lifted it to my nose and was surprised that not only was it real, it was fresh. I returned it to its place.

The service was brief, no more than fifteen minutes, so I assumed the lengthy eulogies and heavy hymns had taken place in the adjacent church. When the crowd began to move, I returned to the truck and waited for him. As I could have predicted, he was last to leave the graveside.

"How was it?"

"Beautiful. Why didn't you come over?"

"I did." I started the engine and put on my seat belt.

"I meant closer."

"I guess because I've heard it all. Plus I didn't know them, so what would be the point?"

He sighed—heavily—and looked out his window as the church and cemetery disappeared beside and then behind us. "You missed a lovely service," he said.

"I heard a few bits of it."

"So you *did* pay attention?"

"Just enough to know it was like most funerals."

"How so?"

"Oh you know. Praise him. He was wonderful. We'll miss him."

"You don't believe that's true?"

"Like I said, I didn't know the guy, Travis, right? I just know the services, the prayers, the preacher, they're all the same."

"Hmm," he said in the universal tone that meant more was coming. "That's not been my experience."

"You've been to a lot of funerals? What are you, my age?"

"I've been to some, yes. Some up close, some from a distance. All are different."

"Not to me."

We cruised out of Fort Valley and back over the mountain into Edinburg. I was confident we'd moved past the stranger's funeral.

We hadn't.

"So, John, did you happen to notice the faces of the people who attended the service today?"

"Can't say so."

"Well I did. And it's a shame you didn't. There was hope in their eyes."

"Hope?"

"Hope and belief. And understanding."

"Looked like a lot of typically sad people to me."

"No question there was sadness. That's natural. But what you didn't see was the joy and the gratitude."

"What were they grateful for?"

"Time. Every day they'd had with their husband, brother, father, and grandfather."

"I guess that's the difference between your funerals and mine. Most of mine have been for people taken from me long before they were ready."

"And who decides when they're ready, John?"

"Fate?" I hadn't meant for it to sound like a question and I immediately corrected it. "Fate."

"You really believe that?"

I didn't hear the question. I was doing math in my head. "Do you know that I had less than ten years, *total*, with my wife? Counting the time we dated before our wedding? If God had let her live to be seventy-six years old, just seventy-six, I would have had sixty years with her. Sixty. Lou Lou would have been fifty-six."

He hung on every word.

"Instead I got nine. Lou Lou got five, probably three of which she won't ever remember. And I didn't even get to hold Willard. Not even once."

He crossed his hands in front of him. "Remind me again how long you had?"

"Nine years with Emma Jane."

"Nine years?"

"Yes, what of it?"

"Almost three thousand three hundred days."

"I guess."

"God created the world in six. Then he gave you three thousand three hundred with his daughter. What a gift."

He may have continued talking, I don't recall, I was seeing how many of our birthdays, anniversaries, and Christmas mornings I could remember.

Every single one.

Twenty-five
Couch Prayers

LOU Lou had the fall flu.

The perky blonde at People's Pharmacy had known our family for long enough to know what we'd been through. She led me around the pharmacy recommending remedies.

"The powders are effective, John, but they don't taste very good."

"But they work?"

"They seem to."

I put both flavors in my basket. On the next shelf over were the cold and cough syrups. I held up a familiar-looking brand.

"Those definitely taste better than they did when we were kids."

I put the grape, berry, and bubblegum flavors in my basket.

"What about these tablet things?"

"They're relatively new, John. And popular. You put one on her tongue and it's meant to melt away. They're made to absorb quickly."

"They taste okay?"

"As good as medicine can taste." She touched my arm to reassure me.

In the basket went the tablets.

I added vitamins, cough drops, a box of tea with a lemon on the front, a new thermometer in case the one at home was broken, a cold compress, a heating pad, and a bag of Skittles. The total was $72.22.

"You might have more than you need, John," she whispered.

"Just playing it safe."

She gave me a sweet and honest you-are-trying-so-hard smile. "Have you called Michelle? I know she'd love to help."

Do I know you? "I haven't yet, but if she's not better in the morning, I will. Thanks for your concern."

She ran my credit card and double-bagged my items.

I looked out the large front window to check on Lou Lou sitting in the front seat of the truck. We'd parked right in front and another pharmacy employee was asked to keep an eye on her. The passenger's-side window was down, and the young woman was holding and admiring the turtle. Lou Lou rested her head on her folded arms, and even from my distance and through a window I could tell her color was still more pasty than peach.

I thanked the pharmacist and walked out.

"John." She stopped me at the door. "If you need anything at all, please call, okay? I'll be here late. And if she's not feeling better by tomorrow night, you might want to call your doctor."

I nodded a thank-you and relieved the helpful young woman outside.

"Any better?" I asked Lou Lou as we pulled into traffic.

She shook her head. Even Shell the turtle was too tired to answer for her.

"Give a look in that smaller bag. There's something that might help."

She dug her hand in and pulled out the family-sized bag of Skittles. A smile.

"See? Take two of those and tell me you don't feel better right away."

She struggled to rip open the package, and when she did, half of it spilled to the floorboards. Then came the tears.

"Oh, Lou Lou, it's alright, shhh."

That didn't work.

"Lou, don't worry about it. It's just candy. We'll get more."

She covered her face with Shell and sobbed.

I could see beads of sweat on her temples.

I pulled into a bank parking lot.

"Lou, what can I do?" I dug nervously through the bag looking for the one thing I already knew I hadn't bought. Tissues. Thankfully there was a stack of clean Arby's napkins in the glove box. "Here you go."

She didn't need them after all. When she pulled Shell from her face, he was the one wet with tears.

"What's wrong, Shell? Are you sick, too?"

Lou Lou didn't smile that time. She continued sniffling and it was obvious she was trying so hard not to start crying again. I wondered if her stomach hurt, too.

I put the back of my hand on her forehead the way I'd seen Emma Jane do. She felt like a frying pan. "Let's take your temperature." I opened the thermometer and stuck it in her mouth.

Lou Lou repositioned it under her tongue.

"Should we go see the doctor?"

She shook her head.

"Let's try these." I opened a package of the cherry-flavored, wafer-looking tablets, placed one in her hand, and heard a beep.

She looked confused.

"It won't hurt you, they taste good."

She still looked confused.

Then I realized Lou Lou had the thermometer in her mouth. "I'll take that." The digital numbers read 101.7.

Lou Lou still hadn't eaten the pink tablet, so I pulled another from the package, held it up, and plopped it in my mouth. "See?"

She put hers in her mouth, too.

"You'll feel better in no time." I drove fast toward the orchard, but was careful on turns and hills. I didn't know why; it just seemed right.

I carried Lou Lou into the house and laid her on the couch. By the time I'd gathered up my portable pharmacy from the truck and returned to the living room, Lou Lou was asleep.

Do I wake her and feed her dinner? Do I wake her and check her fever again? The box says I can give her another tablet in four hours . . . Do I wake her then or wait until morning?

I sat on the end of the couch by her feet and read the rest of the boxes and packaging. "Don't operate machinery?"

Her shoes were still on. I untied them and pulled them off.

"You heard that, right, Lou Lou? No tractors for you."

I slid to the middle cushion of the couch, lifted Lou Lou's feet, and slowly rested them back down on my lap.

Emma Jane loved to have her feet rubbed, especially when she didn't feel well. I was certain if she were there she'd be rubbing Lou Lou's feet.

So I did.

At 8:15—I know because I checked my watch—the phone rang. After four rings the answering machine picked up. The machine took a lot of calls back then.

"John, it's Michelle. Are you there? Please pick up . . . Rosy at the drugstore called, she said Lou Lou's got the flu . . . Please pick up."

The finer points of patient confidentiality weren't my specialty, but something told me Rosy was a rule breaker.

"John? You must be there. . . Rosy said you bought half the cold and flu aisle . . . Are you at the doctor?"

That's the last time, I thought, *that I shop at People's.*

"Please call me. I'll be up late." I thought she'd hung up, but after a few seconds of silence she finished with the words: "Let me help you."

Later I found myself kneeling on the floor. I don't think I'd ever knelt at the couch before. Maybe because the cushions didn't smell very good.

"God, please bless Lou Lou to feel better."

My mind traveled to Baby Willard.

"God, I'm trying, aren't I?"

Emma Jane loved to pray.

"If you're there, if you're listening, please make my little girl feel better. She's all I have left."

What would Emma Jane do?

"Why can't this part be easy, God? Everything else is so hard, can't this be something easy?"

Lou Lou rolled over on the couch, still holding tight to Shell and looking miserable.

I stopped praying aloud.

If you'll make her better, I'll try harder. If you'll get her talking again, maybe even laughing again, I'll try to go back to church. I know I've been away too long, so I'll try, God. Not every week, not at first, but I'll go.

No response.

God, could you at least ask Emma Jane what she would do?

The phone rang again and the machine went back to work.

"John, it's Michelle. Are you there? Why haven't you called?"

Um, God, could you ask Emma Jane what else she would do?

Twenty-six
What If

❧

MICHELLE spent the night on the orchard. She arrived around 10:00 P.M., worried, obviously somewhat panicked, but controlled.

I was impressed that although she gave my coffee-table drugstore a look of shock and awe, she held her tongue. So I didn't debate her when she asked me to carry Lou Lou to her room. I didn't even argue when Michelle said she was going to sit by her bed for a while.

"Get some sleep, John. I'll keep an eye on her."

If losing Emma Jane taught me anything, I'd learned how hard it is to be exhausted, worried, and angry at the same time.

I slept until 9:30.

"I made you breakfast," Michelle said as I appeared in the doorway. The kitchen was bathed in blinding sunlight. I closed my eyes and enjoyed the smell of pancakes.

"You didn't have to do that."

"I know," she said. "But I did." She put a plate in front of my usual place. "Enjoy."

Lou Lou was already at the table, and I kissed the top of her head. "Better this morning?"

Michelle turned around from the stovetop, and I bent down and kissed Lou Lou's head again.

Lou Lou nodded.

"Where's Shell?"

"He's still sleeping," Michelle answered for her. "Isn't that right?"

Lou Lou nodded again and baptized a hot pancake with syrup. Syrup oozed off the side of the plate until there was almost as much on the table.

"Oh dear," Michelle said and was halfway to a rag when I stopped her.

"It's fine. Let it go."

I was pleasantly surprised that she returned to her seat and began eating her own breakfast. She even snickered when I ripped off a piece of my own pancake and dipped it in the mess.

Lou Lou didn't react.

"She slept okay?" I asked.

"Not really, no. She was up quite a few times. You didn't hear?"

"I guess not." I helped myself to another pancake from a platter on the counter.

"I think she should see a doctor, John. Do you have time today?"

"Of course."

"Are you sure, John? I don't mind."

I dipped another strip of pancake in Lou Lou's pool of table syrup. "You've already made an appointment, haven't you?"

"Yes, but only . . . You know I just wasn't sure how long you needed to sleep."

I wiped my mouth with a napkin. "Would you mind taking her for me?"

She hesitated. "Are you sure?"

"It would be a favor, actually."

"Is that alright, dear?" Michelle pulled back Lou Lou's bangs. "Can Grandmother take you to see Dr. Higgins this morning?"

Lou Lou shrugged her tiny shoulders.

We finished our pancakes, I had two more, and Michelle made small talk about work and church.

Bob was busy with a new client from Ashburn.

Their preacher shocked everyone by announcing he was marrying a widow from Conicville.

Bob won an award from some national association of something or other.

Michelle had found a box of baby pictures of Emma Jane. "Would you like to see them?"

"Sure," I said. "That would be nice."

Michelle cleared the table while Lou Lou and I watched cartoons. When she was finished she let Lou Lou have a bubble bath and helped her get ready for their trip to the doctor. "I'll take her to our house after, alright, John? Come get her after your work is done. And stay for dinner, if you like."

"Huh. We'll see."

As soon as Michelle's SUV disappeared down

the hill in the driveway I changed my jeans and T-shirt, put on a denim jacket, and drove to the crosses. Instead of parking I drove by slowly, looking nonchalantly to see if anyone was waiting for me.

I was disappointed to find no one was there.

There hadn't been fresh flowers at the crosses in far too long, at least ten days, so I drove down Route 11 to the florist in Woodstock. The woman there knew me well and respected my privacy. I knew she wouldn't pose a hundred questions or shoot the awkward, sympathetic looks I got most other places.

I bought a dozen white carnations and made the drive north again. This time the clearing wasn't empty.

"Hello, John Bevan." He waved and called to me as soon as I stepped off the road.

"So formal today."

"Just being polite."

I laughed. "You're even polite when you say you're just *being* polite."

"Touché." He shot me with his thumbs up and his index fingers pointed at me like guns, just like my brothers had at the bus stop on Middle Road.

I put the carnations down in the grass in front of Emma Jane's cross.

"None for the other?" he asked.

I felt silly, embarrassed, and ripped the rubber band off the stems. I separated the bouquet and put six back down by Emma Jane's cross and six by Baby Willard's.

"Can I make a suggestion for next time?"

It was another of those questions I was pretty convinced that he wouldn't wait for me to answer.

"Next time bring an extra carnation. White if you can."

"Why?"

He looked down at them. "I just like white carnations."

"Um, okay then." His answer might have seemed strange a month ago. "So where to today?"

He began walking to the road. "How much time do you have?"

"Uh-oh, that's never a good question."

He turned and smiled but didn't clarify. He just kept on walking to the side of the road.

"As much as you need." I began to follow him. "How about that? Weren't expecting me to say that, now were you?"

"No, but I hoped you would."

We loaded into my truck. "Where to?"

"The orchard."

"My orchard?"

"*Your* orchard."

"You want a tour of my orchard?"

"Thank you, I'd love one."

"Well played. To the orchard then."

We chatted on the way about the history of apples in Virginia and how I ended up an

191

orchardist. He was interested in the decision making Scott and I went through after Father's death. Curious how often I saw my brother. Interested in Tim and whether I thought he might have ended up on the orchard someday.

The Cross Gardener had a way of making everything I said interesting. In his presence my stories and ideas were important. *A rare talent,* I thought.

"Here we are." I pulled into the driveway and stopped just shy of the fence.

"Great fence," he said. "I love picket fences. You build it yourself?"

"With my wife, yes."

"Wonderful."

We got out of the truck and I led him down the closest row of apple trees. "There isn't much to see by way of fruit, obviously, because the harvest is over."

He reached down and picked up a rotting apple. "Why are there some on the ground?"

"If it's a mature apple, which that one is, it probably fell during harvest. That happens a lot. Or it could have just fallen from an apple bin. That happens, too."

"How long can it sit on the ground before it starts to rot?"

"Not long in Valley heat, that's for sure."

"And you don't go by and pick them up?" He placed the apple back on the grass.

"Not usually. They can bruise if they fall. And no one wants a bruised apple."

We walked to another row.

"Are all these trees the same?"

"No, we try to alternate rows. A lot of orchards do. That first row was Red Delicious. These are Ginger Golds."

"Ginger Golds. So those aren't red, one assumes?"

"One assumes correct." I smiled. Standing there and looking at his curious eyes, almost childlike, I realized that I hadn't told anyone about my favorite type of apple, or why it was my favorite, in a very long time.

"Ginger Golds are special." I looked to the end of the long row of appleless trees. "They're also the first we harvest. These were picked before Emma Jane, my wife, died."

"I see why they're your favorite then."

"It's not just that, they've always been my favorite apple. The Ginger Gold is a result of Hurricane Camille back in the sixties. Nineteen sixty-nine to be exact. The hurricane about washed away the orchard of a man named Clyde Harvey. Almost nothing left but devastation. Some time later when they were saving what trees they could, they came across a tree Mr. Harvey hadn't ever seen before. It produced a yellow fruit instead of the red on the other trees around it. Eventually they planted more of them and he named it for his wife, Ginger."

"Thus, the Ginger Gold," the Cross Gardener said.

"That's right."

"What a miracle that something so sweet, something that brings joy to many, came from something as tragic as a hurricane. That's lovely. One of the sweetest things I've heard."

I couldn't argue. I'd had my own dreams of one day picking an apple from a tree named for my own Emma Jane. As we walked on to another row I reminded myself I'd forgotten to take the steps to rename the orchard itself. I promised not to forget again.

We walked down another row, then another, and I told him how Father used to roam the rows when the crop wasn't producing as expected. "He said the orchard would tell him how to get the most from it, if he'd only listen."

"Wise man."

We moved to yet another row and I taught him about other varieties. How they tasted. When they were picked. Who bought them. How they were stored. How they were transported. He made the connection to the two crosses he'd shown me off old Route 55 that belonged to the Mexican workers who'd driven a delivery truck for Father.

We walked past the house to the back half of the orchard and eventually up the hill to the highest point. "My grandfather, father, and brother are buried here."

"I assumed," he said. "I'm sorry. It must be hard to lose so many."

"You could say that."

He asked if he could sit.

"Of course."

He sat on one side of the crosses and I crossed around to sit on the other. But we could still see each other's faces clearly between them.

"Tell me about them."

"My family?"

"Yes. If you'd like."

I would, I thought, and so I did. I started with my father's story of inheriting the orchard from his father, a grandfather I'd never met. I told him how my father had been married to a woman who did not believe in him or the orchard and how I'd been adopted just like my two older brothers. I shared how close Tim and Grandpa had become during their short time together.

He was curious about Scott, and I couldn't hide how proud I was of my successful brother.

"You think a lot of him," the Cross Gardener said.

"Oh yes. More than I can say." I felt tears welling up and instinctively shifted the flow of our conversation to him. "How about you? Any brothers?"

"Countless. You, your brothers, your dad, the postman, your workers on the orchard, we're all brothers, correct?"

"I think you know what I meant."

He winked at me. "No, no *earthly* brothers. One sister though."

"Yeah, yeah." I raised a hand. "I get it. We're all God's children."

"You say it like a memorized Sunday-school answer, but not like a truth."

"Who really knows, right?"

"Me."

"I don't doubt you *think* you know."

He lay back on the dying, brown grass and stretched his legs and arms out wide.

I prepared for a sermon.

It didn't come.

I lay back on the grass, too, and was surprised at how quickly it had lost its color and life for the winter. The temperature was cooling, too, and watching a flock of birds form and swoop to the south above us reminded me Halloween was coming fast. One year earlier Lou Lou insisted on going as an apple pie. Emma Jane's mother made the costume by hand with a hula hoop, panty hose, and brown fabric.

"John?"

"Uh-huh."

"Do you believe in God?"

"I guess."

"Do you believe He loves you?"

"I hope so."

He paused a moment.

"Do you believe He loved your wife?"

"Probably more." I said it as a joke, but I didn't mean it that way.

"So you know God loves you. And you know He loves your family."

"Is this a trap?" This time I both *said* and *meant* it as a joke.

He went quiet again.

"What if I told you I know things."

"About?"

"About death."

"You must know something, you're the Cross Gardener, right, friend?"

He leaned onto his side and rested his head on one arm. "What if I told you that I have a gift. A gift of knowing how people died?"

I sat all the way up. "I'd say you know how to read the obituaries."

He smiled before I even finished the line, as if he'd heard it before.

"That's not quite what I mean." He sat all the way up, too, and crossed his legs in front of him. "John, I'm saying it's more than a hobby for me. The way I like to tend and care for crosses and memorials. The way I like to offer comfort, it's more than my life's work. I have a gift, an inexplicable gift, to know how people died and who led them away."

I hopped to my feet. "Okay then, this is getting awkward."

He also stood, much more slowly, and stepped into my personal space. "What if it's true? What if I knew?"

I tried to stand my ground. Protect myself. "I don't know. I'm . . . not so sure what that would mean."

"Why not, John? What if it were possible to have the veil parted ever so slightly? What if some of us could *see* things, *know* things, would you believe?"

The urge in my throat and legs was intense. The urge to slowly back up and surprise him by sprinting down the hill and into my house. But there were questions to ask, and my mind raced faster than my legs ever could.

"What if?" That was all I could say.

"Yes, John Bevan," he answered. "What if."

Twenty-seven
Centreville

THEY weren't requests; they were instructions. "Go inside," the Cross Gardener said. "Get whatever information you can about your mother. Make arrangements for your daughter. I'll wait in the truck."

"Where are we going?"

"I'll wait in the truck."

I walked calmly up the stairs to the porch, opened the door to my home, shut it behind me, and ran to the filing cabinet by my desk. I ignored the wicker basket on top that held bills to pay, papers to sign, errands to run, drawings from Lou Lou to admire.

In the very back of the cabinet I found a hanging file with a manila folder inside. The same manila folder my father gave me as a teenager. It held everything I knew about my mother, her life, my arrival in this world, and later at the orchard.

The phone wasn't in its cradle, and it took me a few minutes to find it under a stack of unopened mail on the counter.

"Hi, Michelle, you're home. How did it go?"

"Just the flu, we think. He gave her a prescription for the cough though. Her lungs are full of mucus."

"Can I talk to her?"

"She's sleeping."

"Oh," my voice fell. My mood did, too. "When should I pick her up?"

"It's up to you, John. But I think she'd be better staying here, just until she's up and has some dinner. But only if—"

"You're right. She should stay."

"You're sure?"

"One hundred percent. In fact, why don't you keep her overnight. I'll get some work done and pick her up in the morning. Do you think she'll be alright for school?"

"Tomorrow's Saturday, John."

"Right."

Awkward pause.

"Go get caught up, John. You must have a lot to do. I'll call you if anything comes up."

I thanked her, genuinely, and hung up.

He was waiting in the truck as promised, or maybe, warned.

"I'll play along," I said, buckling my seat belt, "but I'll need more from you. A lot more." I started the engine.

"That's fair, John. Open the folder," he asked.

I did, and the police report from my mother's accident was right on top, just as it had always been.

"See an address?" He pointed.

"Hers?"

"Yes."

"This one? In Centreville?"

"Let's go."

I turned off the engine. "You want me to drive all the way to Centreville?"

"I could drive, if you'd prefer, but it's *your* truck."

Why am I laughing?

"That's what I like to see," he said. "Let's go."

I started the truck again and drove us to Interstate 81. I got on and took the very next exit for gas at Route 11. As I pulled into the Liberty station I wondered if he knew yet the irony.

Traffic was light going our direction, east on 66, but the westbound traffic from commuters and weekenders was even heavier than usual. We passed Front Royal, Markham, The Plains, Haymarket, and the outbound traffic became heavier by the mile. When we reached Manassas, the traffic had become a parking lot.

"My goodness, I'm glad we're not in that." I looked at the speedometer. We were doing seventy-seven.

"It's quite an image, isn't it?"

"The gridlock?"

"The masses. Look at all those people fighting to go in the same direction. And here we are sailing merrily along against the grain."

We got off at Route 28 in Centreville, but without directions or a GPS I had no option but to pull into a gas station and ask for directions. "Me or you?" I said and pulled into a spot at an Exxon.

"You."

"Why am I not surprised?" I went in and scratched out directions on the back of a gas card application. We were close.

I climbed back into the truck. "Alright. I've bought in so far. But I'm not just pulling up to this place without knowing why."

"Do you trust me? Because, friend, if the answer is 'no' then we have a problem, don't we?"

"I trust you, *friend,* or I wouldn't have just driven seventy-five miles on a lark."

"Then let's go."

"No, no, no, trust doesn't mean closing my eyes. What's your plan? Knock on the door? Ask for the family she was living with when she died? Tell them you used to live there and hope they're having a barbeque in the back?"

He looked stone-faced at me.

"You don't get it, do you?"

He shook his head, and so did I.

"Forget it, just give me some idea what you're hoping to accomplish by pulling up to this place."

"Haven't you always wanted to know?"

"Know what?"

"Who your mother was and how she died?"

"How does parking in her driveway tell me any of that? The people probably don't even live there anymore."

"Maybe. Maybe not," he said.

"Then why? Why are we going?"

"Don't you mean, *what if*?"

Twenty-eight
Listen

THE two-story townhouse was dirty tan with dark brown shutters.

We pulled into an empty space on Forest Pond Court directly in front of the address on the police report. The yard was overgrown and weeds had escaped through the sidewalk cracks leading to seven concrete steps and a concrete porch with no railing. A single shade tree stood to the right of the porch. Had it provided shade back then?

Two dead bushes sat on either side of the final step up. They once stood proud guard, I imagined, greeting my mother each day she left for school or work. Maybe they worried the day she drove off for the last time. They might have been the last to see her alive.

But no more. On that day they begged to be dug up and tossed in a landfill.

"Now what? Waltz up and knock on the door? See if my old man lives here?"

"That's your choice, but I say we go home."

I whipped my head around. "What?"

"Do you trust me?"

Here we go.

"Because if you do, you'll look a final time and begin the drive home."

"Seriously? And sit in that traffic? Drive all the way in to look at the front yard and its dead bushes? Are you kidding?" I got out of the truck and slammed the door behind me for effect. I also mumbled something but I don't think he heard it. I walked bravely up the walk, just like my brothers would have.

I stood at the door.

There was movement inside. Someone was barking at a dog to get off the couch. Footsteps clunked down stairs that sounded like they ended right inside the door.

The doorbell was broken and taped over with a torn half-strip of duct tape. In black Sharpie on the tape someone had written: KNOCK HARD. "Hard" was underlined.

I wanted so badly to turn around to see if the strange man, the game player, the Cross Gardener was watching. I finally did, but he wasn't. He was staring out his open window, looking across the parking lot at nothing in particular. I pulled both hands from my pockets, held them together, and blew into them. It wasn't that cold.

I rubbed my left earlobe.

What will I say if the man still lives in this townhouse he owned more than twenty years ago?

What if he has my eyes?

What if he recognizes me? What if he's always known where I ended up? What if?

I listened to the noise behind the door and put my fist against it. I'd never wanted to hit anything so hard in my entire life. Not when a punk named Teddy made passes at my sweetheart, not when Tim died, not even when my father died. Certainly not when Emma Jane and my baby died; I'd been too numb.

But in that moment on that porch guarded by two dead bushes, I wanted to knock until the door fell down.

I listened. The noise stopped and was replaced by a humble whisper. Real, imagined, audible, it didn't matter. Emma Jane's voice was as clear as the first time she'd said the words. "Don't, but I love that you would."

I stuck my hands back in my pockets and walked down the steps, down the sidewalk, over the weeds, and got into the truck.

I prayed he wouldn't say anything.

He must have been listening. All he did was point to the police officer's narrative description of the day my mother died.

Sunday. 1976 Ford Pinto. Troubled young woman. Drove south on 29, then west on 66 past the battlefields of Manassas and Gainesville. Light rain.

I started the truck and drove south on 29, then west on 66. Sitting in the parking lot of Friday evening traffic, I finally found the courage to speak.

"You knew I wouldn't knock, didn't you?"

He looked at me, maybe through me. "No."

"But you hoped?"

He smiled.

We slugged along with the traffic, windows still down, the sounds of life filling the car and my imagination.

"John?"

"Yeah."

"Do you know what the hardest skill is for human beings to learn?"

"Isn't it obvious? Forgiveness."

"That's a skill?"

I took my eyes off the road to look at his face. "Not for me."

He nodded his head a moment. "I was thinking of *listening*. That's a crucial skill, don't you think?"

"I guess it could be."

"Are you a good listener, John?"

"I think so."

"Does your daughter think you're a good listener?"

I looked at him again and nearly rear-ended the car in front of us. "What?"

"If I asked her, would she say you're a good listener?"

"I heard you." I rolled our windows up with the electronic window switch on my door panel.

"Maybe not always," I offered. "But she knows I try."

"Would you like to practice?"

"Practice listening? Don't you think I've been listening a lot to you today? And last time? And the time before that?"

"You have, and I've enjoyed the conversation. But what if I could tell you more?"

"If I listened?"

His eyes said, "Yes."

I considered his implication for a moment and then answered with my own eyes. "Alright."

Then came the silence. Inside the car. Outside. The space we occupied together became peace. Not just peaceful, but actual peace.

The truck still rolled along. Faces still passed us on their way home. My hands were on the wheel and landmarks my mother must have passed that night appeared in the foreground, then next to me, then behind, then gone.

I listened.

"What if your mother was calm the night she died?"

I'm listening.

"What if instead of a scared young woman, more young than a woman, she was coming to strength? The man she thought she loved wasn't much of a man at all. He was twice her age with half her courage. Not a bad man, but a broken one."

My passenger stopped talking. I think. It could have been seconds, even minutes.

"What if your mother wasn't running *from* something that night. What if she was running *to* something? What if instead of gathering her will and instead of practicing the next steps, she was displaying her will? Displaying her steps? She was no longer a student, but was a graceful ballet dancer on a grand stage, all alone for the first time in a dangerous and new routine. God, traffic, her baby, they all saw a new woman that night in the rain . . . Rain that turned to freezing . . . Roads that became dangerous . . . Her speed unsafe."

Listening.

"What if it wasn't an accident, John?"

I looked at the Cross Gardener. I was hearing him, but I wasn't sure he was talking out loud anymore.

"What if God, your Heavenly Father, your literal creator, knew this was coming? What if it was part of a grander plan? Did He know how your mother's earthly life would end? Did He see the accident? Was she frightened? Was He there and did He comfort her? Or did someone else?"

There were other questions, and I'd heard every one. Some more than once. Some I'd asked myself long before our evening drive together.

I have no memory of taking the exit, but we'd arrived at the top of the ramp of Exit 298 in

Strasburg, just as she had. Route 11. It was dark now. A light rain fell.

I didn't need him to tell me to turn left.

One hundred feet, two hundred, three hundred.

"Pull over."

We parked in a shopping center under construction.

"It happened here."

I got out of the truck.

He followed.

"This was nothing back then, just fields and scattered trees. Your mother was in the far lane. The crash happened here." He walked into the street and stood on the double yellow line. "Impact."

Listening.

"No one thought to plant a cross for her back then, much less garden one. But if they had, it would have been there where you stand. But no one came to mourn here."

What about her friend? I thought. *The girl she lived with?*

"Not all suffering has a cross, does it?" He walked out of the road and stood by me. "There was grief in the home she left that night. Guilt, too. It wasn't me, of course, but I know she had a Cross Gardener of her own. Someone who comforted the suffering ninety miles away in a small townhouse in the city."

A car sped past us and honked in ignorance.

I took a few steps backward.

He didn't follow. Instead he turned around to face me.

"You want more."

Yes, I thought, *how does he hear me?*

"Did she die alone?" He asked my question.

I'm listening.

"She did not die alone, John. As always, in every single case, someone was there to greet her and introduce her to the other side of the veil."

Who?

"A strong woman. A woman she admired more than any other."

Who?

"A graceful mentor with an eye for potential."

My mind drew the image of a missing gym bag with two pairs of ballet shoes and an overdue library book.

"It was her instructor, John. And I promise you the instruction never ended, it just moved to a different stage."

Twenty-nine
The Window

HOW did he know I'd be there?

I'd adjusted my Sunday circuit that day. I visited the crosses on the orchard, left four white carnations, dropped Lou Lou at Bob and

Michelle's for church, skipped the drive to Woodstock, had gone to say hello to Emma Jane and Baby Willard on Route 11, left three white carnations, and driven out John Marshall Highway—Route 55—toward Front Royal and Panorama Memorial Gardens.

The cemetery was quiet. The pond in front was not. Winds nipped and ripped at the surface of the water and leaves raced from one side to the other, stopped in spots by lily pads that swayed on their strong tethers.

I pulled past the caretaker's house and followed the lane back to the sparsely populated section that held captive Emma Jane and my baby. The closest grave was at least twenty feet away, and there were lots of other vacancies between the north edge of the cemetery and us.

I sat. The ground between Emma Jane and Willard's brass-and-granite marker wasn't as comfortable as my place at their memorials on Route 11. I framed the marker by placing one carnation horizontally along the top and another on each side.

"I'm here," I said. "Are you?"

The wind from the pond found me.

"Emma Jane, what's happened?"

I whisked away a fly from Willard's engraved name.

"What's happened to the life you promised me?"

A car drove behind and around me toward the

other section, and an old man waved through his rolled-up window.

"This isn't what I agreed to, Emma Jane. I miss you. And I'm not very good at being sad."

A Warren County fire truck cruised by without lights, sirens, or hurry.

"She misses you, too," I continued. "Our sweet, sweet Lou Lou. I hardly recognize her. Do you see how she's taking her time stepping into our new life? I'm trying to be there for her, but I'm not very good at that either."

A red minivan passed behind me with little faces watching me through every window but the driver's. One tiny face smiled. And though the windows were tinted, I thought I saw a small bouquet of balloons in the back fighting to get out the back door.

"Willard, or Baby Wil, I'm sure we would have called you Wil, we miss you, too. We think of you every day."

What would you have looked like? I thought. *Would you have been tall? Would your baby blue eyes have stayed blue? The orchard would have been yours someday. Did you want it? Or were your dreams like your uncle Scott's? Life in the city and a courtroom, or a sky-rise office building, maybe you would have gone to Wall Street? Or been a teacher like your mother wanted to be? Maybe a doctor? A firefighter at the station in Woodstock?*

"Emma Jane, I've met the most fascinating person. A man with the strangest ideas. He calls himself a kind of caretaker, a Cross Gardener. He tends to memorials across the Valley, including yours. He is a comfort to be around, but an odd one. He has gifts, I am sure. Wisdom. Like a pastor. He says he talks to God and God listens. I think, maybe, maybe God even talks back. He says my mother did not die alone the night I was born. She was greeted—" I looked around to be sure no one was watching or within earshot. I was alone, but I began talking more quietly anyway. "He says that the woman who taught my mother to dance led her through the light. What do you think of it? Am I crazy? Is he?"

I wanted Emma Jane's opinion at that moment more than I'd ever wanted anything. But she didn't answer.

"I think you would have liked this man."

I continued to talk, ramble mostly, about my days and about my nights. The times I woke up smiling because I'd dreamt of us at the river kissing in a canoe when her parents got too far ahead and couldn't see. Or the times I woke up crying because my dream took me to her grave and I banged with an angry fist on the ground like a man knocking on a heavy wooden door. But she did not answer.

She listened to me itemize my loss. My mother, Tim, the men from the orchard, Father, Grandpa

Bevan, Emma Jane, our son. *Has anyone been asked to suffer so much?*

I practiced listening.

The wind took my gaze over my shoulder to a single bench and a single tree not far away. How did he know I'd be there?

He didn't look at me until I was close enough to take a seat next to him.

I did.

"Hello."

"Happy Sabbath," he answered.

"Are you gardening today?" I asked.

"You tell me."

His hands were in his lap. I'd never looked so closely at them. His skin was so smooth compared to mine. *Hands of a thinker,* I thought, *not an orchardist.*

"How long have you been here?" I asked.

"Not long."

I glanced at my truck and turned to face him. "So if my truck is there, and I came alone, who did you hitchhike with *this* time?" I grinned.

"Mom."

"Of course. You do pay for gas, right?"

He laughed. "I care for her, she cares for me. We're a good team."

"That's nice." I privately wondered if my mother and I would have gotten along and cared for one another the way my friend and his mother did.

We listened to the wind blow in and out of the tree next to us. The minivan I'd seen drove by again and the kids still had their noses plastered against the glass. I surveyed the cemetery and saw a bundle of balloons tied to a cross some hundred yards away, at one of the nearest graves to the mausoleum. The van passed the pond and ventured onto Route 55.

"May I make an observation?" he asked.

"Isn't that why you came?"

He didn't answer.

"Yes," I added, sincerely, "please."

"Your life is a most interesting series of symbols. Have you ever seen it? Your father's workers died on Route 55 many miles to the north. You live just off the same road. Your wife and child's bodies are buried here in a cemetery off 55."

"I've thought of that, sure."

"And your wife and son died on Route 11 on one end of Strasburg, and your mother died on the other end of Strasburg, also on Route 11."

"Uh-huh."

"I bet from the air it looks like a cross."

Now that I hadn't thought of.

"Curious," he closed.

The wind slowed, not completely, but to the point it didn't pay attention to you, you had to pay attention to it.

I took a turn. "May I make an observation now?"

"Please."

"You know so much. Some of it obvious, or because I've told you, or just . . . because. But I know so little about you."

"A fair point. What would you like to know?"

Where do I start?

"When you're not here, or tending to crosses, what do you do?"

"Tend to other crosses."

"You know what I mean . . . when you're not doing this, your passion, when you're just living like everyone else, what do you do? Where? Do you have friends? Other hobbies? Did you go to high school around here? Are you married? Kids?"

He tried to keep a straight and serious expression, but it soon cracked into laughter. "Where did all *that* come from?" He cackled the question.

"Wow, I don't really know myself. Just all bottled up I guess."

He continued laughing. "I'm not quite certain where to begin."

"Pick one."

"Alright then. I'm from the Valley, but I travel and I've moved around. I like to travel. I love people. People are my hobby, I guess. I'm a people watcher, too. The people around me fascinate me. Like you—"

"People watcher, that explains a lot." I cracked.

"And I love to learn. Not in a classroom per se,

216

but in life. I won't end my day without learning something."

"Did you go to SHS?"

"Strasburg High? No."

"College?"

"No, I didn't graduate, but I've done a lot of advanced course work."

"In?"

"Theology, mostly, but also physiology."

"So you don't have a day job, right? Family money then?"

"We have what we need, but we're not rich, no. We survive."

"Family?"

"I have a sister, I told you that already, but I've never been married."

"Would you?"

He seemed to struggle a moment before answering, and I was tempted to apologize for the personal question, but I chose to listen instead.

"I think so, yes. I could see myself getting married." He turned the tables. "What about you, John. Would you remarry?"

The question seemed too fast, inappropriately early. I hadn't for a single slice of time considered the question. But now I did.

"That was too personal, I am sorry."

"No. It's alright." I stood up and zipped up my jacket. "I don't think so, my friend. I don't think so."

"What if she wanted you to?"

"She?"

"Your wife, John. What if she wanted you to find love again?"

A familiar SUV pulled into the cemetery and made the turn toward us. "Let's go."

He followed me in a fast walk to the truck. We drove away before the other vehicle could have seen us, or even known which grave we were visiting.

"Stop," the Cross Gardener said from the passenger's seat.

"Those are my in-laws, they don't need to see me here."

"I know. Just stop over there." He pointed to a tall Christus in a loop in the road. "Park there a moment. I want to show you something."

"You don't get it? I don't want to be seen."

"Trust me."

I parked in the loop that circled the statue of Christ above a much smaller mausoleum, only a few feet off the ground. We watched as Bob and Michelle got out of their vehicle. I was embarrassed when Bob opened the back door and Lou Lou got out. I'd forgotten she was with them. Maybe I'd forgotten it was Sunday altogether.

Lou Lou was wearing her prettiest Sunday dress. The one her grandparents kept in a closet in the room they called hers.

Bob was in a dark suit, Michelle in a fashionable skirt and blouse with a heavy wool jacket. *Too heavy,* I thought, *for late October in Virginia.*

"Why are we sitting here?" I asked.

"Just sit and watch."

"You know we can't leave now until they do, right?"

"John, you need to see this."

"See what? They probably come every week."

"Watch," he persisted. "And listen."

Bob held Michelle's hand and they walked toward the grave in short, careful steps, as if on ice they feared would crack.

Michelle watched the ground.

Bob watched her.

Lou Lou and Shell walked a few steps behind.

They stopped at the grave, and Michelle tucked her head into Bob's chest. He wrapped his arms tightly around her. From my view it was calm, completely controlled.

Lou Lou sat on the ground with Shell and pulled something from his backpack. It looked like paper dolls she'd made in school.

The image could have been a brochure for the cemetery.

Until Michelle collapsed on her knees.

Bob immediately knelt beside her and rewrapped her in his arms. I don't know if I could hear the deep sobs or just knew they were coming from her anguished face.

Lou Lou watched from her safe place on the ground until Bob beckoned her closer with a flick of his fingers. She crawled across the grave and both grandparents gathered her up.

I looked through their window.

I listened.

For the first time ever I heard pain that didn't belong to me.

Thirty
For the Best

I should have seen it coming.

Scott called me November 1st. Lou Lou had been feeling better, but when I asked if she wanted to trick-or-treat on Halloween night, she said no. I pulled out the costume Emma Jane had made the year before and thought it might entice her. But it's possible she could tell I just wanted to see her try it on again.

"You don't want to go at all? Not even to Grandma and Grandpa's neighborhood?"

Shell raised his left hand.

"Would Shell like to go instead?"

He raised his left hand again.

"You don't have to, Lou. It's your choice. But I know Grandma and Grandpa would love to see you in your apple-pie costume."

Four hours later she fell asleep watching *Troll 2* with me on the couch.

At 8:00 A.M. the phone woke me up.

"Hey, John."

"Scott? What time is it?"

"After eight, you're still asleep?"

"It's Saturday. The world is still asleep."

"Not my world, brother."

"Glad I live in the Valley then and you're an hour away."

"Actually, that's why I'm calling. Can I come see you today?"

"Sure. Why?"

"Hang out. See Lou. I haven't seen her in forever."

"Alright. We're around all day."

"You got the fertilizer on yet?" Scott asked.

"No, soon though."

"Huh."

There was another question in there, but he must have decided to save it.

"So what time will you be out here?"

"Half an hour."

"What?! Where are you?"

"Somewhere on 66."

"Thanks for the heads up. What if I had plans?"

"Yeah right."

"Yeah right," I mocked. "Fine. I'll be up. Bring donuts."

"Deal."

"See you—"

"Wait, John? April's with me, is that okay?"

"Super, now I have to shower, too."

We hung up and I checked on Lou Lou. She was still asleep and I pulled her door shut.

A long shower, shave, brushed teeth, clean jeans, a JMU sweatshirt. As I pulled it over my head I heard the front door open. "Where's my little brother?" he called.

"Shhh," I said, walking down the hall. "Lou Lou's still asleep."

Scott motioned with his balding head to follow him outside. I did, and April was just walking up the steps.

"Hey, April." I met her at the top stair, and she gave me a friendly, long hug.

"How have you been?" she asked.

"Alright, I guess."

"Good." She released me from the hug but kept a hand on my back. "You look good."

"You, too. Still have bad taste in men?"

"The. Worst."

Scott punched me in the arm. "We have evidence to the contrary."

"Oh yeah?" I said.

"Show him."

April held up her left hand. The ring was so big I was surprised she could lift her hand at all.

"Really?"

"Really!" she yipped, and I initiated the hug this time.

"Congrats, guys, that's great." I punched Scott back, much harder than he had. I think. "Took you long enough."

"Whatever." He rubbed his bicep. "Not all of us find our soul mates in high school."

You could have heard a rotten apple drop ten rows away.

"Man, I'm sorry." Scott covered his eyes with one hand. "I wasn't thinking."

"Shut up, yeah you were, and you're a million percent right. Emma Jane and I just knew, we always knew, and we knew we were lucky that way."

"She *was* lucky, no doubt about that." April tugged on the sleeve of my sweatshirt.

"You two have a date yet?"

"Next spring, probably in May."

"Or April." She giggled.

"So precious." I giggled back.

"April." Scott became serious. "Would you check on Lou Lou? John and I are going for a walk."

She squeezed in between us and through the front door.

"Seriously, Scott, congrats, that's great news. What a nice girl."

"Thank you," he said. "Truly. It's been a long time coming. You remember the first time you met her?"

"Of course. My own wedding."

"That's right," he said.

"She was the second-prettiest girl there."

Scott stepped off the porch. "Let's walk."

We circled the house, went through the back gate in the picket fence, and up the hill to the clearing.

"It looks nice." Scott ran his hand along Tim's cross.

"Been a while since you've been up here?" I asked.

"I'm afraid so."

I sat on the ground near Father's grave.

"How about you? You get up here often?"

"I dunno," I lied. "Occasionally."

"The crosses look freshly painted."

"Yeah, I try to keep them up."

Scott sat in almost the same place my friend had on his last visit. He looked down to the rows of trees below. "Do you remember how he walked this place over and over?"

"I do."

"If those trees could talk, right?"

It was a question without need of a reply. So I didn't give one.

"So, John, there's something else I wanted to talk about."

"Uh-oh."

He shifted his weight.

"What's up?"

"I'm curious how you're *really* doing."

"I'm alright. I said that already."

"Come on, John."

"I am, why? Does something look wrong?"

"I call you three times to get one call back. And do you even check your e-mail anymore? I bought you a thousand-dollar laptop because I thought you'd use it."

"Really? This is about a computer? Or not calling back fast enough? Scott, I'm doing fine."

"How about Lou Lou?"

"She's the same."

"Same?"

"No worse." I took a quick breath. "She's a little better every day."

Scott uncrossed and recrossed his legs.

"What's this about?" I pressed.

"The Elkingtons."

I should have seen it coming, I thought.

"Bob and Michelle are worried."

"Not about me, I'm guessing."

"Yes, naturally they're concerned about you. You and Lou both."

I shook my head for some time before speaking again. "We're fine, Scott. They've tried this before. They asked me back in September if Lou could stay with them for a while. I put my foot down."

"How so?"

"What do you mean 'how so'? I said no way. She'd be better with me trying to work through this. They kept screaming at me that she needed routine and consistency and blah blah blah but then wanted to take her off the orchard and raise her in their home? I said no way."

"How has Lou been since then?"

"Better."

"How so?"

I took to my feet. "Scott, are you here for some reason? Did they send you here?"

"Absolutely not."

"Did they call you?"

He hesitated.

"They called you? And said what? Get out there before John ruins her? Convince him to let us keep her?"

He stood, too, but kept his distance. "That's not what happened, John, but yes they called. Concerned. She got really sick—thanks for not calling me by the way—and she spent time there, right?"

"So?"

"So she started to feel better, talk a little, and then got back to the orchard and regressed."

"Regressed? Who are you anyway?"

"I'm your brother and I'm helping. John, don't walk off. You need to listen."

Listen.

"Look around, John. The orchard is hurting. Harvest was a disaster. Have you seen the numbers I sent? The guys who covered the accounts said it was the worst harvest they've seen in years."

When had my brother ever sounded so tender?

"The orchard needs you."

I looked away and down the hill toward the house.

"Did you go out last night? Did you both go out for Halloween?"

Just listen.

"She said she didn't feel well, right? You stayed up late instead? Listen to me, John, your daughter is not well right now. Six-year-olds don't skip Halloween because they don't feel good."

He took two steps toward me.

"Brother, she's sad. It's going to take time for it to fade, and no one says you're not trying, but we all believe it might happen faster with Emma Jane's parents."

Two more steps.

"Nothing permanent, just a break for both of you. Some time to heal. The Elkingtons say you can go anytime, eat dinner there. Shoot, eat *all* your meals there if you want. But let her stay awhile, John."

My hands and knees were shaking. "Why?"

"I just told you."

"No, Scott, I mean why couldn't you let me get to this point by myself? If ever?"

"Would it matter?"

Would it matter? I thought. "I just needed a

little more time, Scott. I would have done what's right for her on my own."

"I know you would have, brother. But this is why I'm here. This is my job now, it's been my job since Tim left. And since Dad left. I'll do anything for you. And today, I'm protecting you."

"Just a little more time, Scott. I was trying."

He took two more steps, put a hand on my shoulder, and when he saw me beginning to cry, pulled me into his arms and protected me as well as he could. "It's for the best."

Thirty-one
Alone

🙢

JUST another Sunday morning.

Except that it was the Sunday after the Saturday that Scott and April had come with good news and a hammer. But, unlike every other week, I did not get to pick her up on Sunday evening and bring her back to the orchard.

I dropped her off and left a duffel bag with much more than I'd ever sent her with, and more than she probably needed. It wasn't heavy, but it felt like carrying a casket all by myself. I also left a note for the school giving Lou Lou permission to ride the bus home to their house, even though they promised to pick her up every day it was feasible. That note felt almost as heavy as the duffel bag.

After the customary small talk, I bent down to Lou Lou's level and grabbed both her hands in mine.

Michelle politely withdrew when she realized these were the final good-byes.

I watched and waited until she'd shut the door behind her.

"You're okay with this, right, Lou Lou?"

Shell raised his right hand.

"How about Shell, is he okay with it, too?"

This time Shell didn't raise a furry green arm, he nodded.

"Oh! Shell is nodding now? How cool. He's added something to his bag of tricks."

She unzipped Shell's brown backpack and pulled out the pink bunny she'd won at the fair the night her mother and brother were killed. But when she tried to hand it to me, I put my hands behind my back.

"No, no, no, you don't. I can't take care of that thing."

She shoved him in my chest.

"Are you sure? What if he gets out of the house and hops around the orchard? Gets lost? Gets married to one of the neighbor bunnies? That's a lot of responsibility!"

Ten weeks ago she would have answered, "Oh, Daddy, you're a silly sack of apples. It's just a stuffed rabbit!" But it wasn't ten weeks ago; she just half-smiled. Still, the light in her eyes—dim as it may have been—was enough to make the pain of knives in my stomach and back easier to absorb.

"I'll miss you, Lou. Be safe. Listen to Grandma and Grandpa, okay?"

She hugged me around the neck and put her tender face in the nape of my neck.

I could tell she was crying.

"This is a good idea. It really is. Even though it doesn't feel like it right now. But it's hard for me, too . . . I just know they're going to take such good care of you."

She switched from one side of my neck to the other.

"Have fun, promise?"

I felt her nod.

After a few minutes of enjoying the silence and being alone, the door opened and Michelle reappeared. I saw Bob standing behind her and keeping his distance.

I pried Lou Lou's arms from around me.

"Sweetheart," said Michelle, "Grandpa is making a pie for tonight. Do you want to go help?"

She looked to me for permission, which I only granted after a final hug and kiss. I kissed Shell, too, and that actually made me feel better.

A final squeeze of her hand. *I love you.* I said it silently with three squeezes.

I love you, too. She answered with four and walked off.

As I stood and straightened up, Michelle met me with her arms open. And before I could think or decide if I wanted a hug, I was in one.

"We love you, John."

I listened.

"It hurts now, I know it does, but this is for the best. If we didn't think so, we wouldn't have suggested it."

You did more than suggest it, I thought. *You orchestrated it.*

I lowered my arms.

She didn't.

So I raised them again out of courtesy and resumed the embrace.

"You're like a son to us, John. Do you know that?"

I didn't answer. Not because I didn't want to, but because I didn't know.

She finally pulled her head off my shoulder and looked at me, but her arms remained locked on my back. "She'll always be yours, John. They'll *both* always be yours."

"Thank you," I finally managed.

Those two simple words flooded her eyes with fat tears. She pulled me all the way back in again. "We love you." She raised her voice for the rest, as if someone were listening and she needed them to hear. "Get whatever help you need, John. And take care of the orchard. You need one another."

She kissed me on the cheek, and I said good-bye.

The first week alone passed like those summer Sundays in church. Even though I ate dinner with Lou Lou and the Elkingtons every night, I drove home to an empty orchard. I practically prayed for a Spanish-speaking picker to park on my grass, just for the conversation.

I visited the university extension to find out how the harvest had been across the region. Good for some, average for most, bad for me. It seemed everyone knew I'd been AWOL.

I visited Emma Jane's and Willard's crosses. The Cross Gardener wasn't there.

I got a haircut.

I paid some of the bills sitting in the wicker basket.

I visited the cemetery. The Cross Gardener wasn't there, either.

I spent time on the tractor spreading mouse bait.

I walked the rows to feel less alone.

I whispered apologies to whomever was in charge of providing answers.

I called Scott back.

I turned the nursery into just another room.

I downloaded 843 e-mails, most of which offered to improve my life with a degree, an influx of cash from some foreign captive, or porn.

I deleted them all. The e-mails from Scott and a few high school friends were dumped into a folder I titled FOR LATER.

I returned a call to the bank.

I paid some more bills.

I visited the crosses on the orchard. No Cross Gardener.

I drove to McCauley and cleaned up litter that had been thrown near the memorial for our Mexican workers. When there wasn't a bottle or cigarette butt within twenty feet, I expanded my cleanup perimeter until I couldn't even see the bridge they'd crashed into anymore. I examined the crosses closely, just in case, but they didn't yet need to be touched up. I decided to leave the paint in the truck for next time.

I noticed the fence I built with Emma Jane needed a new coat of paint. Only one side of the fence got done though, because I knew Lou Lou would want a turn painting, too.

I went back to the crosses on Route 11. Nothing.

I drove and sat in the truck at the exact spot where he'd told me my mother had perished. Nothing.

I got out of the truck and walked to the double yellow line where she'd seen truck grilles and bright lights. Nothing.

Never in my life, not since the night I came into the world and my mother left, had I ever felt so alone.

Thirty-two
The List

❦

IT had a cross and a dove stitched in white thread on the front.

I'd never planned on writing in it again. It was her journal, not mine, and even cracking the cover felt like stepping beyond some line I'd promised never to cross. But when I did pull open the leather cover, I felt so close to her. It was the last of several journals on the shelf; the one she was slowly filling when the truck killed her in August.

The entries I read that night at the kitchen table weren't soul shaking. But the way Emma Jane wrote. The careful, trained cursive. The perfect curls and loops. It was the handwriting of a teacher. The words themselves didn't move me, but the fact that they were *her* words did.

I ran my fingertips along the page because I knew one day she had, too.

Each page deserved to be perused, respected. I liked that Emma Jane had not written every single day, but not a single week passed without at least one entry. Some days were quick bursts of thought, probably on nights I was annoyed the lights were still on because the orchard had taken everything I had that day. Those entries hurt.

Most of the pages held simple thoughts, and I'd not realized the extent to which she loved making lists.

Things to make for Christmas.
Things to thank my parents for before they die.
Things to teach Lou about being a woman.
Things to try in the classroom.
My favorite teachers.
Things I remember from Sandy Hook Elementary.
Favorite books.
Places to go with John before we die.
Things I love about the orchard.
Things I love about God.
Promises I've made.

I went to a blank page and decided to make my own numbered list. I took a pencil from her night-stand drawer. It had a red apple as an eraser.

THINGS I MISS ABOUT LOU LOU:
1. Her being on the orchard.
2. Her laugh.
3. Seeing her on the couch eating cereal.
4. Letting her ride in the front seat of the truck.
5. Watching cartoons with her.
6. Watching anything with her.
7. Tucking her in.
8. Tucking Shell in next to her.

9. Watching her color.
10. Watching her sleep.
11. Her eyes.
12. The way she doesn't wink very well.
13. Sitting on my lap on the tractor.
14. Standing at the bus stop.
15. Standing behind the line at the bus stop.
16. Waving at me.
17. Watching Shell wave at me.
18. Shopping at Food Lion.
19. Holding my hand when we visit Grandpa Bevan, my father, and Tim on the orchard.
20. Sleeping in the backseat of the truck when she's tired.
21. Seeing me at the door at the in-laws when I pick her up.
22. How nice she looks on Sundays.
23. Her just being here.
24. I miss Lou Lou.

I closed the journal and walked back to our bedroom. I lay down on Emma Jane's side of the bed and held the journal against my chest.

Another list came to mind, one I'd thought of every day since burying Emma Jane and Willard. I shared it with God.

"Father in Heaven, or God, or Creator, or whatever it is I'm supposed to call You. I'm praying now."

He didn't answer.

"When I was born you took my mother, Libby Riffey. My father, biological father that is, was never there to be taken away."

I paused for a moment and listened. The house was perfectly quiet, like the anxious moment before a newborn cries for the first time. No wind. No cars. Black silence.

"Before I even met him you took my Grandpa Bevan. When I was nine you took my big brother, Tim. Then you took my real father before I was ready, before any one of us was ready."

I slid the journal up to my nose and mouth and breathed in. "Then you took Willard from me. A baby. An innocent little baby. For what? All those months in Emma Jane, for what?"

I lay still until the quiet returned.

"Then the worst of all was taking my Emma Jane. The only girl I ever loved and the only woman who ever, ever loved me back. She was it, God, she was *the only one*."

I opened the journal again and began reading. Her entries, my entries, the list of things I missed about Lou Lou. I read the list again. Then again. It was all true, I missed it all.

"God, I miss her."

Who? I thought.

"My daughter, of course."

Thirty-three
Ocean City

I'D taken the complete Sunday circuit.

My friend at the florist in Woodstock made four small fall flower arrangements for me. She'd throw in the extra white carnations for free.

Grandpa Bevan, Tim, Father, my mother, the fairgrounds, Route 11. I even pulled in front of the ugly blue house on the east side of Main Street in Woodstock. Emma Jane pointed it out to me every time we passed, as if I'd never seen it. "It's just so . . . so *blue*," she always said. "I just love it."

If they ever painted that house, I'd show up in the night in a ski mask and overalls and paint it back.

I drove north out of town. My heart used to race when I approached the place of impact and the clearing on the right. Not anymore. Now it just beat. *Thump-thump, thump-thump.* Just another stretch of road. *Thump-thump, thump-thump.* Driven it a million times. *Thump-thump.*

There he was.

The Cross Gardener.

It couldn't have beat any faster without ripping from my chest and speeding down the road.

I skipped the parking spot down the road and pulled right into the clearing.

He was painting again.

"There you are," I greeted from the open window of the truck.

"And here *you* are." He took a final stroke across the thin edge of Baby Willard's cross and set the brush down.

I asked what I'd been wondering all week. "Where have you been?"

"Working."

"Hmm, I didn't think you worked."

He cocked his head to the right. "You didn't think you were the only one who needed help, did you?"

Sometimes it feels that way, I thought.

"Of course not."

"Good. But I'm glad you're here. I need a ride."

I hid my excitement as best I could. "I've got some time, it's Sunday."

He loaded the paint can and brush in the back of the truck, and we popped out of the clearing and into the light weekend traffic.

"You can go any direction you want, but I suggest 66 into D.C., then 50 east across the bridge."

"To where?"

"Ocean City, Maryland."

"I wondered."

"You knew I'd take you there?" he asked.

"I hoped."

We rolled the windows down and enjoyed the unseasonably warm November afternoon. Interstate 81 had its usual load of semitrucks, always heavier on Sundays than any other day of the week. Route 66 carried in the weekenders and day-trip tourists. When we neared the Capital Beltway I remembered Scott telling me the Washington Redskins had a bye week. So traffic was light and moving at the speed limit, an unusual but welcome blessing.

We veered onto Route 50 and crossed into Maryland. The bridge to Ocean City swayed beneath us, and when we reached solid ground on the east side my mind was starting to sort through the questions I wanted—*expected*—answers to.

The final miles and minutes ticked by in conversation that started trivially enough.

"How's your daughter?"

"You can call her Lou, or Lou Lou if you like."

"Alright. How's Lou Lou?"

"She's forging ahead. Staying at her grandparents right now."

"I see."

Out of the blue I thought of another thing to add to my list of things I missed about her.

"It's just temporary."

He stuck his hand out the window and let the wind blow between his outstretched fingers. "I bet she's doing wonderfully, John."

"I hope you're right."

"I am." He smiled but didn't turn his attention away from the fun he was having out the window.

I admired his childlike innocence, so easily amused, so eager to please.

"Has it been hard on the orchard without her?"

You're kidding, I thought. "You could say that."

He inhaled and exhaled loudly. "I'm sorry to hear that."

I asked, "Do you mind if we roll up the windows? It's gotten a little chilly."

"Not at all."

A mileage sign passed and it hit me how close we were. Had he sensed it?

"John, may I ask when was the last time you were here?"

"Ocean City?"

"Yes."

"The day Tim died. He drowned in the morning; we were here by late afternoon." I remembered sitting in the lobby of his hotel and watching Father stoically process the news. "We spent one night and drove home the next morning. His body arrived that day sometime at the funeral home . . . I think . . . It's been a lot of years."

Another mileage sign. The numbers shrank and my anxiety grew. We drove in silence until I rolled our windows back down and the smell of the sea filled the truck.

He breathed in again, filling every nook and cranny of his lungs. "I love that smell."

241

I filled my lungs, too. The smell reminded me of Tim.

At the south end of the boardwalk a Ferris wheel and roller coaster watched over the coast. The carousel, the boardwalk fries, the games. All of it made it impossible to think of anything other than the Shenandoah County Fair.

He led me down the stairs from the boardwalk to the beach. He removed his shoes and let his feet sink into the sand. His eyes were wide and happy.

I did the same.

"Come on." We strolled down to the water and he pointed to the north. Side by side we walked at the edge of the water, the point where the sand was cold and wet. Hard. Every three or four steps another wave petered out under our feet. I know it was three or four because he was counting.

Then he stopped and pointed to a hotel. "They stayed there, didn't they?"

I wasn't completely sure; there were so many hotels and many of them looked newer than the one his senior class must have stayed in over twenty years earlier. "Follow me." It was my turn to lead.

We walked back up the beach, slipped our shoes back on, crossed the boardwalk, and entered the beachfront lobby entrance. The memory was as obvious as the sand in my shoes. The couch I sat on with Scott was gone, but another sat in the same corner of the lobby. The tile floor was the same. The check-in counters in the same place. The pillars probably repainted but unmoved. Because the holidays were approaching, someone had wrapped garland around them from floor to high ceiling.

We stood in the lobby in the same spot I saw a principal cry and my father gather facts from a police officer.

"This is it. How did you know?"

"You must have told me."

Really?

"My turn again." He led me back out the door and down the same path to the beach. Again the shoes came off. But this time his shirt did, too.

I didn't want to think. Mine came off, too.

"Are you ready?" he asked.

"Yes."

"Run." He turned and began to run down the beach, arms above him, head looking toward the heavens, wind blowing through his hair. He jumped the first wave, then the second. The third swallowed him.

I rushed right in behind him, afraid that stopping to consider all the reasons not to would be another mistake I'd carry forever.

The water took my breath away. Literally. It was so cold I couldn't breathe.

"John!" he yelled. "Come farther."

I dipped my head under a crashing wave almost

as tall as I was and popped out on the other side. When I tried to put my feet down to regain my balance, they flailed below me.

"Farther," he called again.

When I got to him he was on his back doing the dead man's float. "Welcome," he said like a dinner-party host.

My teeth were chattering.

His were not.

"This is insanity," I chattered.

"Lie on your back."

It was dusk now. The sea and light bathed us the way it must have on the morning Tim left.

"Isn't it a miracle?" he said.

"What?" I was slowly adjusting to the water. Or becoming numb. In the moment it was hard to tell.

"Here we are. A different day, a different time of day, a different season even. But it looks just like it did when Tim passed."

Small waves, not yet fully developed by the power of the current below, bobbed our bodies up and down in the fast-fading light.

"Your brother loved to be in the water. But he wasn't a very good swimmer, was he?"

"No, he wasn't."

"But the water was mysterious, it was an unknown challenge. Your brother sought challenge, didn't he?"

It's time to listen, I thought.

"He woke up that morning feeling restless. Graduation was near, the bounds of being a child nearly gone, he was older than his age hinted. Bravery. Maturity. Readiness. He felt it all that morning."

I turned to look at the shore. The boardwalk lights were drifting farther and farther away. No part of me was frightened.

"He snuck out of his hotel room and walked casually through the lobby. He wore cutoff jean shorts and a tank top. He wore tennis shoes with no socks, because he hated the feel of flip-flops."

The ocean was quiet, the waves crashing on the shore a distant soundtrack, like the pickers' stereo across the orchard. Audible, but indistinguishable from the sounds of chance and nature.

"Tim sat on the sand first. Took his shoes off. Smiled at a couple of shell hunters walking past and leaving two sets of footprints behind. He considered the months ahead. Leaving your father and the home he'd known most of his life. He once told your father that the orchard was his heaven, and if he didn't make it to the real one, at least he'd know what it looked like."

I shivered and my eyes filled with salty tears.

"He removed his tank top and jogged into the surf. Like us, he jumped some waves, dove under some others. Shortly he found himself swimming well beyond the waves, where the water was as smooth as the Atlantic ever gets."

He stopped for a moment. It was getting quite dark, but when he continued, I wasn't sure his lips were moving. It didn't matter, I heard him perfectly.

Tim had it all, he continued. *He had options. He turned to his back and floated just like this, just like you and I. He looked at the sky and wondered if the clouds would look the same when he was lying on his back under a tree in Africa. Or Australia. Or Madagascar. Tim could picture a group of would-be hunters gathered around, hanging on his every word, waiting for his next move. Just like the water that carried him farther and farther from the safety of shore, they would react whenever he moved a muscle.*

A large patch of seaweed squeezed between us. I turned again to look for the shore. The lights from the hotels and boardwalk were dots now. The ocean could have been a mile deep beneath us. The stars lit the water around us, but without the lights of the shore we'd never find our way back. My instincts said to panic. My soul said to keep listening.

John, your brother thought of you. You must know that.

Why would he have thought of me? I thought.

He worried about you and Scott on the orchard. John, he worried so much about his youngest brother, the one so new to the orchard. He hoped Scott would, in time, protect you as well as he had.

Scott has protected me well.

Tim also worried about your father. Because Tim had a fear, an oft-recurring fear, that something would happen to him while he was exploring his dreams off the orchard. And who would care for the land and the brothers he loved so much?

Please, I'm ready to know, who led him home?

He continued. *Still on his back, Tim became nervous when two jellyfish oozed by him. He began to tread water and kept his eyes focused on the shore. Then another jellyfish came too close, and another, and he paddled faster toward the shore. The faster he paddled, the less distance he covered.*

I heard him clearly, but my thoughts were singular. *Who led him home?*

Tim's thoughts turned to his father. The man he never even met. The man who walked out on his life and Tim's mother when she was still only weeks pregnant. He wondered what kind of man he was eighteen years later. Would he still have walked out if he'd known then the kind of man Tim would become? More jellyfish threatened, and Tim was in an unfamiliar place. Real fear. His natural instincts wanted to call out for a mother he'd not seen since the nursery in the hospital. She'd walked out, too, but not because she didn't want to raise him. She walked out because she knew she couldn't raise him. He'd been put up for adoption, which, for reasons I do not know, produced a terrible environment for him. In time he landed at the orchard. He was led there.

I rolled my legs under me and began treading water.

The Cross Gardener did the same and we watched one another.

"Who led him home?" I asked.

"Tim succumbed to the panic, the fear of the jellyfish around him, and ran out of breath. His head dipped below the water and he gasped for air. He came up fully, but slipped beneath the water's heavy blanket twice more, his arms flailing wildly above his head. Even at that moment, knowing the end had come, Tim understood the jellyfish hadn't killed him, fear had. . . . Then after his last breath, he learned the universal lesson: No one dies alone. Tim watched as a strong arm reached down and pulled him to safety. But it did not pull his body; it only pulled his soul."

"Who?"

"It was the man who taught your father everything about apples, life, lines, and family. The one who passed the orchard to your father. The original orchardist. Tim's grandfather, your Grandpa Bevan. He was Tim's personal Cross Gardener. *He* led him home."

My shivering stopped. I put my head down and swam to the shore.

Thirty-four
One Crash, No Cross

I felt like a piece of wet bread.

For some reason he dried off more quickly than I did, and I knew the seats in my truck would smell like the ocean for a long time. But I didn't mind.

We drove home the way we'd come. I stopped for food and gas, and it soon looked like my passenger had dozed off. But when I leaned forward to look more closely, I saw his eyes were open.

"Tired?" I said.

"No, just at peace."

The words made me smile. Wasn't he always at peace?

I had a thousand and one more questions than when I woke up that Sunday morning and took my Sunday circuit around the Valley. There were answers I knew he had for me, or at least hoped he had for me.

Quiet never felt so comfortable. We rode along, windows back down with crisp air rushing through my window, across the cab, and out his.

"I have one more stop," he said after we passed the second Front Royal exit and neared the 81/66 split.

"Where?"

"Just drive."

Two more miles and we had no choice but to go north or south on Interstate 81. Route 66 had come to an end.

"South, then there." He pointed to the side of the road just past the split. I put on my hazard lights and came to a stop on the right shoulder just before the road became a ramp to the south.

I turned off the engine. "There's nothing here."

"Follow me." He got out of the truck and began walking down the right side ramp against the guardrail.

I wished I had a flashlight, but even with one I was sure I wouldn't see a memorial. I'd been over the ramp thousands of times. There were none.

"Here." He stopped by a newer-looking section of guardrail and put his hands out in front of him. "Come."

I stepped out of the road toward him.

"Years ago," he began, "it's not important how many, a man died here."

"But—"

"He wasn't speeding or intoxicated. He wasn't forced from the road by an inconsiderate driver. He was simply tired."

I looked more closely along the ground by the guardrail.

"He was driving home to Buena Vista, Virginia. Another one hundred twenty miles to go. It was 2:12 A.M. The man had been gone for just a week at meetings in New Jersey. Only a week. But he missed his wife and five children dearly. The idea of another night in a hotel when he was so close was out of the question. There were no mobile phones, no option for checking in but an inconvenient pit stop at a pay phone. Frankly, he was afraid a call home would end with his sweetheart insisting he stop at the nearest motel and sleep."

The Cross Gardener sat on the guardrail and gestured for me to join him. A Walmart semitruck rumbled past.

"He'd made a decision that if he were tired by the time he reached Harrisonburg, he'd get off the interstate for a cup of coffee and a phone call."

"He never made it."

"No. He began to drift asleep and when his VW brushed the left guardrail, he overcorrected and crashed into the right. Five minutes passed before the first car approached the scene. He pulled over and almost immediately another vehicle arrived. The second was dispatched to find a pay phone, the closest being Strasburg. Not only had the man passed away before the rescue squad arrived, but his body was already cooling and vacant."

"Was he afraid?"

"He was not. He knew with certainty where he was going."

"Who met him?"

"His childhood idol. The scoutmaster of his Boy Scout troop."

I thought, *What comfort.*

Another vehicle passed. A tow truck.

"John, you noticed there's no memorial."

"I did. Why bring me here then?"

"The man's family received his body the next day in southern Virginia. They held a service at their church and buried him in a cemetery in Roanoke. Months later the widow drove the children to the city to visit their aunt in Alexandria. She passed this spot and suspected it was the one by the brand-new piece of guardrail. But she didn't stop. She didn't even tell her children."

"Why not?"

"Because it didn't matter."

His death didn't matter?

"The *place* didn't matter. They visited once, they even left flowers, but after time and prayer, their individual choice was that the precise place wasn't relevant. Even though their personal preference was to mourn differently, they still honor those who do choose to plant roadside crosses. And every time they pass another memorial they whisper a prayer, both for their own father, and for the unknown victim remembered there. It is their way."

"And now?"

"I know that two years later she found another

man who loved her and accepted her children. He cared for her and she had love again. Now, John, she missed her first husband, the father of her children, and she thought of him every day. But she did it differently. She went to the cemetery on holidays, taught the children who he was and what he stood for. And she built a new life with the wonderful man who took her in. She moved on. Not necessarily away from her first husband, just forward."

He knew my next question.

"There is no wrong way, John. There is only *your* way."

Thirty-five
The Balloon View

HAD he slept on my couch? When I awoke sometime after 10:00 A.M. the next morning, the Cross Gardener was sitting on my front porch in the chair that used to be Emma Jane's.

"Good morning," I said and sat next to him. I rubbed the remnants of sleep and disbelief from my eyes.

"You slept well," he said without breaking his rocking chair rhythm.

"Was that a question?"

"No, I could tell you had." He looked at me and smiled big.

I rubbed my entire face this time. I desperately needed a shave and shower. I could still taste the salt on my lips. "What a night." For a moment I'd considered that the trip to Ocean City and back had been a dream, but my sandy tennis shoes on the porch by the front door convinced me otherwise.

We rocked back and forth, at times in sync. "Is it Monday?" I asked.

"I don't know."

I stopped rocking and chuckled at him. "What a nice life you must lead. Never having to wonder what day it is. How good it must be, huh?"

He pointed his eyes and words right at my chest. "Isn't that exactly how you've been living your life?"

I began rocking again and waited for him to apologize.

He didn't.

I looked tree by tree through the orchard around me. It needed my time, and I made a promise to give some before the sun set that day.

When I'd finally tucked my pride away, I asked him the first thing I'd thought of when I opened my eyes in bed that morning. "How long will I feel this way?"

He didn't reply immediately. In fact, he didn't reply at all until I asked again a minute later. "How long?"

He rose from his rocker and walked, barefoot, off the porch to the white picket fence. "I have admired your fence."

"I know."

"It's so well constructed, John."

"Thanks, I guess. I had help."

"Who?"

"My father helped some, mostly with design to be sure I didn't screw anything up too badly. Of course Emma Jane helped paint."

"It's quite lovely."

It would have been an odd phrase from most men I knew. Not him.

"Thanks," I answered. "I worked hard on it. It's important to me."

He nodded at me and began to walk toward the closest row of trees.

"You don't want to walk through the orchard without shoes." But he kept on walking. I followed in my sweatpants and T-shirt and realized I wasn't wearing shoes either. "Wait up." I scampered to catch him. "Seriously, walking through here with bare feet can be painful. Just ask Lou Lou."

"Hmm, maybe I will."

We took deliberate steps through the high grass. Mowing was one of the first things I should have done after the harvest. Mow, apply herbicides, spread the mouse bait, prune. I could do it all in my sleep, except that I hadn't yet.

He pulled down a branch of a Ginger Gold tree and examined the end. "John, what do you love most about apple farming?"

"All of it."

"That's not entirely true, is it?"

"Sure I do."

"You love it all? The pruning, spraying, sorting, sweating, selling, driving, men parking on your front yard?"

He had me. "Fair enough. I love *most* of it."

"But what above the rest, John?"

I also pulled a branch down and studied it. "Selfishly, I guess, I love knowing that there's nothing on this tree right now, not a single fruit, but if I make the right decisions and spray the right things on the right days, if I prune it during the winter, next year I'll have an orchard full of apples again. Enough to support my family."

"You think that's selfish?"

"Maybe."

His face was wise. "It's not. The trees are here for you, John, not the other way around . . . How long before fruit reappears after the winter?"

"That depends on the type of apple and how well it's cared for. Some take more time to grow and mature into a ripe fruit."

"Fascinating."

We walked to the end of the row and circled back up another. Twice I stepped on a mushy apple buried in the grass and laughed to myself.

"You haven't been out here barefoot in a while have you?"

"Probably never," I said and thought back. "Maybe when I was a kid."

We arrived back at the driveway, which now separated us from the house. I tiptoed across the gravel.

I returned to the porch first. He took his time getting back, even stopping to admire the fence yet again.

Finally he sat back in Emma Jane's rocker. "I'm sorry, what was your question?"

I leaned back against the rocking chair and shook my head. From my peripheral vision, I could see him looking at me and grinning.

"You're too much, Mr. Cross Gardener."

"Too much for what?"

"It's an expression," I said. "You know, too much for me, too much to believe."

There we were, rocking again and listening to the post-harvest quiet.

"You realize I still don't know your name?"

"My name? Isn't my name what people call me?"

I defended, "Well, no—"

"What's your daughter's name?" he interrupted.

"You know it's Lou Lou."

"So that's her name?"

"Well, no, it's what we call her."

"Aaaah," he said and he was right.

I knew it; he knew it.

"My name is the Cross Gardener. It's special to me because it defines my mission. But you may call me whatever you like."

But I was stuck back on the word *mission*.

"Mission?"

"Mission. Calling. Assignment. They're all the same to me. It's what I'm meant to do."

"Interesting."

"What are you meant to do, John Bevan?"

"Be an orchardist, I guess."

"A fine mission," he said. "Will there be more?"

I shrugged.

"There will be."

We sat like old friends, friends with history, friends who didn't need to talk to communicate. But that didn't stop him for long.

"It's all going to be alright, John."

Is it? I thought and hoped for much more.

"It is. I've seen so much suffering, John. More than you can imagine. Here on the orchard, at your crosses, at others, in the Valley and beyond. I know it's going to be okay because I've seen the other side."

"Go on."

"My head tells me you need me to say this, though my heart tells me you know already . . . It's okay to cry, John. Everyone who cries recovers. It's alright to be sad, even mad, downright angry for a short time. Those emotions can heal, too. Just not by themselves."

"With all due respect, and I *do* respect you and what you do, the pain I feel now feels no different than the pain of October or September. Some days it consumes me."

"Just some days? Of course it does. When you got married, *love* consumed you. When you had a child, love and the need to *nurture* consumed you. When you found Emma Jane was pregnant with another eternal soul, you were consumed with joy and the instinct to *protect*." He breathed.

"And . . ."

"And now you've buried your wife, your true love, and your son. Your daughter lives in shock and guilt. You fear you'll lose her emotionally, even physically, and you are once again *consumed*."

"And yet you tell me it will all be okay. This will pass."

"Will you get fruit again next year?"

"I will."

"Then it will pass."

Another handful of peaceful moments and a healthy gust of air brushed between us and around the porch.

"You know things," I said. "This gift. It is real?"

"Do *you* think it is real?"

"I do." The answer, and the speed with which I gave it, surprised me.

"Then it *is* real."

I stopped rocking and placed my feet firmly on the porch. "When can I know the rest?"

"When you're ready."

"When will I be ready?"

"You'll know."

I began rocking again. "This gift, this special vision you seem to have. Can it tell me who led others besides my family?"

"Perhaps. But it's not to be abused." His voice was kind, but firm. "Try me," he eased up.

My mind rewound to dusty memories, things seen and others only read about. September 11th. Lincoln. JFK. The Civil War.

"All those people murdered, what happened to them?"

"They died, John."

"But what was it like? You said you know things about the process. So tell me. Who led all those people?"

He tapped his fingers on the armrests of the rocking chair. "Cross Gardeners."

"Even those who take lives?"

"Everyone."

"Murderers? Rapists? Warlords?"

"No one dies alone. It is an eternal promise, John, and it comes before judgment."

"So all these Cross Gardeners. They're everywhere? They know when they're needed?"

"Naturally. They are readied and prepared for the day."

"The battles that took place here around us during the Civil War. Each soldier, no matter which side he fought on, no matter his rank, talent, religion, each had a Gardener to make it easier?"

"Of—"

"Hold on. And they were just standing around? Thousands of them?"

"Standing? I don't know. But yes. They knew."

I sat a little straighter. "What do you mean they knew?"

"I mean *God* knew."

"He knows exactly when things will happen? Or did happen?"

"Most naturally. He has said He is the Alpha and the Omega, the Beginning and the End. He sees things you *don't* see, like a puzzle that's always assembled. It's not just seeing the future, it's *knowing* it because with Him there is no past, present, and future. His time is not our time. Understood?"

Not exactly, I thought.

"John, have you ever been in a hot-air balloon?"

"Yeah, actually, I have."

"When?"

"At our senior prom Emma Jane won a ride in a raffle. A few weeks later we went up on a Saturday afternoon in a ride across the Valley."

"Perfect. What do you remember of it?"

"It was amazing." I smiled at the memory. I hadn't thought of that day since long before the crash. "The view was like nothing I'd ever seen. Just amazing. Breathtaking, that's how Emma Jane put it."

"I can imagine . . . Now, do you remember how far you could see?"

I closed my eyes and began rocking again. "The sky was blue, no haze anywhere, we could see as far as our eyes allowed."

"How far is that?" he asked.

"Not far enough."

"When you and Emma Jane were up there, did you spin around and see the entire Valley?"

"Of course. Many times."

"Could you see it all at the same time?"

"No way. We only saw what was in front of us."

"Yes!" He took a dramatic pause, at least I thought it was dramatic, and I repeated my last line in my head.

"That's how He sees the world, John. But He never has to turn around."

"I get that, He's above it all so He sees it all. The grand view. That's no big secret if you believe in God."

"That's only half of the principle. Because if He were in that balloon, He doesn't just see the present view from all angles, He sees it at *all times.*"

I'm listening.

"From the balloon He would see the Valley when only animals flew or scurried about the earth. He would see it when soldiers for the North and South fought for freedom. And He would also see it with a commerce-creating Interstate cutting right through the middle and connecting the North and South."

"Huh." I should have offered something more profound, but *huh* was all that came out. "Huh." I said it again.

"He sees it all. All angles, all times, all intentions. And trust me when I tell you this moment in your life, it's a speck in your journey. And not just this fleeting pain, John, but your entire life. It's just an inch on a glorious ruler that has no end."

I had my mouth half open when he stopped me with a raised hand. "Keep listening, John. If He saw the war, He saw it before soldiers from the North and South were even born. And that, by extension, means He saw those who would comfort them at death. They were prepared."

I drove the conversation back to its beginning. Actually, I did a lot of driving back then. "So, to my question. The people killed, no matter how they died or how good they were, they all had someone?"

"Yes."

"Each and every one?"

"Yes."

"Someone they knew?"

"Not always, but always someone they were glad to see, and always someone who could bring the light."

"Fascinating."

"Like I've said, John. No one dies alone. No one ever has."

Thirty-six
Sand and Skates

I dropped him off at the crosses. When I got out of the truck, too, he stopped me.

"Not today, John."

"Excuse me?"

"Not today. Go work the orchard. Go find your daughter."

His assertiveness should have sent me off balance. It didn't.

"What are you going to do?"

"Do some gardening." He pointed to the clearing. "I'll care for those passing through, you care for the living."

"What if Lou Lou isn't ready for me?"

"She will be."

"How do you know?"

"Because you're starting to listen."

I pressed. "And if she doesn't say anything?"

"Listen harder." He smiled and began to walk away.

"And then what?"

"Talk to God." He turned around a final time. "And listen."

I turned around in the middle of the road and drove straight to the Elkingtons.

Both cars were in the driveway, which surprised me since it was a Monday, and nearly made me second-guess my courage. I walked up the side-walk and stepped up to the front door. But the laughter I heard sounded like it was coming from outside. I circled around the left side of the house and on my tiptoes peered over the six-foot wooden privacy fence.

It was another parent-teacher-conference moment.

Lou Lou was rolling around on the spacious concrete patio in the backyard wearing Rollerblades. She was also wearing a helmet, kneepads, and elbow pads.

Most important, she was laughing. "I'm doing it!" she squealed.

"Yes, you are, sweetheart!" Bob yelled and ran alongside her. "Look at you!"

Michelle held a video camera from a patio chair.

"I'm really doing it!"

I hadn't heard that many words in two months.

There was another item to add to my list of things I missed about Lou Lou. I turned my back and stepped away from the fence.

Did He see this moment before I got here? He must have. Does He also know what comes next? He does. I think I was answering the questions myself. *I'm here because I should be.*

I walked back to the fence and peeked over again. Lou Lou had taken a seat by her grandmother, and Bob was retying the laces on one of her Rollerblades. He tickled her knee and she laughed some more.

I was probably back in the truck with the engine running before Lou Lou was back on her feet again. If I'd asked it to, the truck would have driven me back to the crosses without a thought.

My right shoe felt loose and when I pulled it off the gas pedal and into the light under the steering wheel, I saw sand covering the floorboard. I looked at the radio. Sand. I looked at the door handles. Sand.

My mind saw Tim being pulled to everlasting safety.

The Cross Gardener was kneeling beside a pair of crosses so I didn't have to.

I turned off the truck and walked with long bold steps back to the fence. If only Michelle had caught the moment on camera.

"Daddy!"

Days and weeks later I would hear that word

ringing in my head. Not repeated in different tones or different moods, but in that exact moment.

She rolled to the edge of the patio and clopped across the grass to me. When she struggled to open the gate, I reached my own hand over the top and unlatched it myself. I stole a glance at Bob and Michelle. They were neither surprised nor concerned.

Bob waved.

Michelle smiled and led Bob in the house by the hand.

I held Lou Lou in my arms and lifted her off the ground. When I spun her around she kicked the fence with the wheels on her Rollerblades and giggled.

Ten minutes later when I walked in the back sliding glass door, Bob and Michelle were pretending to look busy in the kitchen.

"I'm going to take her to Stoney Creek."

"Skating? All the way to Woodstock? But it's a school night, John."

"Michelle, he's taking her."

I could have kissed Bob. I didn't.

Michelle looked at him, then back at me.

Lou Lou was already pulling her skates off and putting on tennis shoes.

"The truck's open, Lou, will you wait for me?"

"I'll walk her out," Bob said. "Here, sweetheart, I'll carry your skates for you." She handed them to him and they walked through the living room to the front door.

Michelle waited until she heard it close behind them. "John, be careful."

"Skating?" As soon as I said it I took a deep breath and made the most important decision so far that day.

"I'm listening."

"Only in the last couple of days has she started opening up. The counselor suggested the skates. We had no idea how badly she'd wanted them. But look at her. I think they remind her of her mother."

I smiled, not forced or for show, but because I was happy.

"She's trying, John."

A hug was all I could think to do. She was wiping tears from her eyes when I let her go and said good-bye.

I think I ran to the truck.

Through the window I saw Lou Lou buckled in the backseat; Shell was buckled next to her in the middle lap belt.

Bob shook my hand on the sidewalk. "Do you remember your first date with my daughter?"

I looked at the front door and smiled so broadly Michelle could probably see my teeth from her spot between the living room drapes. "Yes, sir, I do."

"I wasn't sure I trusted you then."

Listening.

He *wanted* to say more. He'd *planned* to say more, I could tell.

He didn't. He just shook my hand again with both of his and walked away. When he got halfway up the walk, I saw the gap in the living room drapes fall closed.

We got on the interstate and made our way south to Stoney Creek. Just past the Toms Brook exit traffic slowed from seventy to forty within a quarter mile. Lou Lou unbuckled Shell and pulled him to her lap.

"It's going to be nothing, Lou. Nothing at all."

Traffic slowed even further, but at least we were moving. Three miles later, now traveling at thirty miles per hour, I looked in the rearview mirror at Lou Lou. She was mouthing something. Probably a prayer.

When I looked up, traffic had come to a complete stop. I slammed on the brakes and barely avoided rear-ending a purple Geo Prizm in front of me.

Stopped.

"Climb up here, darling."

She was halfway over the front seat already. She settled in right next to me.

"This is life on the highway, isn't it?" I looked at her, but her eyes were fixed on whatever had crippled traffic ahead.

"This happens a lot, sadly. But, Lou, it's usually

not serious. People get flat tires, people run out of gas, there are even accidents, but most times, truly, everyone walks away from them."

She was actually trembling.

"One of your mother's best friends lives on up the road in Woodstock, right off the highway. Maybe she pointed her house out to you? Or took you there?"

Lou Lou finally nodded.

"Mom's friend says she stands on their deck all the time and looks over the highway to see something going on. Crazy things, but things that usually don't end so badly . . . In fact, she saw a bear once run right across the road. Can you believe that?"

Her eyes were interested.

"It rumbled right in front of her when she was driving home one day. What would you do if you saw a bear running in the road?"

She said the words quietly without the laughter that drew us together back at her grandparents. "I'd run, too, Daddy."

"That's right. Me, too."

A single Virginia State Police car sped down the emergency lane with its lights firing and siren wailing. I slid her even closer to me.

We sat and waited.

I tried my best to listen.

"Lou," I started simple. "Do you remember your mother's accident?"

She nodded once.

"Was it the saddest day of your life?"

She nodded again, just once.

"Me, too. I get so sad when I think of it."

Lou's gaze began to wander.

"Darling, do you think it was your fault?"

Lou Lou gave me the most painful shrug I've ever seen in my life.

I caught my breath. "It wasn't. It absolutely wasn't."

She began to sniffle.

"Lou Lou, listen to me. It happened because she was needed somewhere else. I promise you she's so busy right now. And probably your brother, too. They have jobs to do."

"Jobs?" Her voice cracked.

"Well sure. They're working for God."

She looked up at me with tears already at the bottoms of her cheeks. The questions poured out. "Are you still mad at me?"

"Of course not. I *never* was."

"Did Mommy hurt a lot?"

"No, darling, she didn't."

"Was she scared?"

"Not when she passed on, Lou Lou, not when she passed."

"Is she in heaven with Baby Willard?"

"I don't know if she's in heaven yet or not, but I know she will be there someday."

She let out a deep breath she'd been holding in

for almost three months. Her voice was weak but faithful. "So will we, Daddy."

And with that the traffic began moving again. It wasn't long before we passed a semitruck on its side. Its load had spilled and covered most of the right lane. The driver stood near his rig, upset but safe. An officer filled out a report. Two others were laughing by their patrol car.

There were punctured and torn landscaping bags everywhere. There's only one place I'd ever seen that much sand: the beach.

Two hours later I dropped off an exhausted Lou Lou at her grandparents' house.

"Can't I come home with you tonight?"

"Not yet, darling."

"Soon?" she said with fresh tears forming.

"Soon. I promise."

Thirty-seven
The Invitation

IT came on a Friday afternoon.

"Can I speak to Scott Bevan, please?"

The secretary put me on hold.

As soon as I heard Scott take a breath to say hello, I flipped the switch. "You've set a date?"

"I thought I might hear from you today."

"I should drive in there and pound on you."

"You wish."

"So seriously, this is how I find out? An invitation in the mail? And who's the balding guy in the photo? He looks like a young Mr. Clean."

"Oh don't pretend to be mad, little brother. What were you going to do, come and help April pick stationery?"

"Maybe."

"Right. And *you'll* get a hole in one before *I* will."

We both laughed.

"I'm so happy for you guys. Honestly, I couldn't be happier."

"Truly?"

"Truly."

Scott rambled on about plans for the winter wedding. The church April selected, her family, the house and its restored threshold that he planned to carry her over after the honeymoon to Ireland.

"You'll be my best man, of course."

"Is that a threat?"

"Nice! No, it's a most humble request."

"I'd be honored."

"Oh, and April wants to ask herself, but just so you know, she wants Lou Lou to be the flower girl."

I already couldn't wait to see her in action. "Hey, this says February, what happened to spring? I thought she was eyeballing the month of April?"

"What can I say? She loves me more than she loves the gimmick. I told her I didn't want to wait anymore . . . Did I tell you she wants to start having kids right away?"

Even though we were on the phone, I could tell he was grimacing and probably rubbing his bald head.

"Good, why wait? You're not getting any younger. What are you, fifty?"

"What are you," he countered, "adopted?"

"Why, yes, how did you know?" We hadn't shared that childish and childhood joke in years, and Emma Jane always slugged me when she overheard it. But at that moment the words sent me playfully running down the driveway to catch a school bus and waiting in blind obedience behind a line drawn deep in the gravel. Not blind because my eyes were closed, blind because I trusted.

I switched the phone from one ear to the other. It sounded like he may have done the same.

"So Sunday's the day?" he asked.

"I think so."

"Are you ready?"

"I will be. All the tractors are working. The entire orchard has been mowed. The pruning is back on schedule. The house is clean and the fridge is full. I even painted Lou Lou's room."

"Green?"

"Of course. And I bought her a real turtle."

"Softie," he jabbed. "How about the rest of it?"
I knew what he meant. "Rest of what?"
"The rest of *you*. You up for it all?"
"I think so. I miss her so much, Scott. I didn't think I could miss someone that much."
We both mumbled *I love you* and hung up.

Thirty-eight
Answers

I did the Sunday circuit for the last time.

The highest point on the orchard, the spot of Virginia clay that had held three crosses so patiently for so long. I left an extra white carnation and said I'd be back sometime soon.

The crash site of my mother, Libby Riffey, on Route 11 where a strip mall now sits. I left an extra white carnation and said I would think of her when I passed, but would not stop.

The fairgrounds in Woodstock where Emma Jane last breathed the clean Valley air. I walked where the big blue slide would stand the next August and couldn't wait to race Lou Lou.

Main Street in Woodstock. The crazy book-club ladies were sitting outside the café again. I waved.

I looked down Court Street at the firehouse that had meant so much and predicted even more.

The ugly blue house at the edge of downtown. Ben Franklin. The County Park. Maurertown. Toms Brook.

The spot I killed a deer.

The spot Emma Jane and Baby Willard passed away.

I knew I'd be a while, so I parked down 11 at my usual spot. I walked back to the clearing and stepped off the shoulder and into the grass.

He was waiting for me in slacks, a white shirt, and dark tie.

"You knew I'd be here," he said. "Didn't you?"

"I hoped."

He invited me to sit on one side of the crosses.

He sat where he'd sat so many times before. "Where have you been?" he began.

"Living." I smiled, but only to mask the nervous energy.

"And?"

"And listening," I acknowledged.

"I knew you would."

A car crawled by so slowly that I turned to look. It was Lou Lou's teacher, Kerri Silvious. I waved and she waved back. I made a note to visit her later and say *Thank you*.

There seemed no point in delaying the purpose of the now-sacred meeting. After all, Lou Lou was expecting me. "I need to know," I blurted.

The Cross Gardener took a deep breath and

nodded his head, as if he were the one bracing for truth. "I'll tell you what I can."

I went to a familiar question. "Is it real?"

So did he. "Do *you* think it's real?"

"I do."

"Then it is."

A predictable beginning.

We watched each other and when his eyes allowed it, I began. "Who led my father home?"

"You mean who is his Cross Gardener?"

"Yes."

"Someone unexpected."

"Who?"

"A man who had his orchards destroyed by forces of nature, but found great joy in the recovery. A man whose wife once called the miraculous discovery 'A gift from God.'"

"The Ginger Gold."

"That's right. Mr. Clyde Harvey."

Something I couldn't have guessed with another year of visits seemed as obvious as the two crosses staring at me from the ground.

"Mr. Harvey was honored to lead your father home."

"Why not his own father? Why not Grandpa Bevan?"

"I don't know, John. But I suspect he was there, waiting in the wings with Tim. But this wasn't his cross to garden."

I had my first tears of the day fighting for

space on my eyelashes. "Where are they now?"

"I'm not certain, but I know they're closer than you think. And I know your father continues to visit orchards. When difficult questions need answers on hot summer days or early fall mornings during harvest, he is there to whisper them."

I'd felt pride before for my accomplished father, my loving, forgiving father, but never like that. The news was sweeter than any harvest had ever been.

"I think I've heard those whispers," I said.

His deliberate nod said, *Of course you have.* The Cross Gardener watched me with brilliant delight.

"You know my next question," I said.

"I do. I've been listening to you ask it silently since the day we met."

Then who?

"John, have you ever noticed that sometimes the answer is the first one you think of?"

And?

"If your wife could have handpicked someone to lead her from this life to the next . . . who would it have been?"

"My father."

He didn't say a word; he didn't have to. I heard him perfectly.

"Do you know how much Emma Jane loved your father?"

"I think so."

"Emma Jane believed that without your father, you wouldn't have ever gotten married. She credits him more than anyone else with your success as a man and a husband. Emma Jane believes it was all orchestrated by a loving Heavenly Father. The crash in Strasburg, the failed adoptions, your arrival at the orchard on Middle Road just miles from where you entered this earth. Your generous father's unconditional acceptance."

"How do you know all this?"

"You want to know what she's doing now? She's teaching."

"Teaching what?"

"Teaching all those who never knew God. There are so many, John, literally countless souls who never knew Him on earth, but have a chance to learn of Him above."

I am completely without words.

"It is her mission, John. And there are many like her."

So she's not here? I thought. *She's never been here?*

"No, John. I'm sorry. She is not a Cross Gardener. It is neither her calling, nor her choice."

Not her choice? The admission filled me with even more questions. *Will I see her again?*

"She hopes so . . . but remember, John, you are not alone, and you never have been. Everyone standing at a busy roadside memorial or kneeling in a quiet cemetery isn't alone either."

"She's close?"

"Closer than you think."

"Willard?"

"Much closer than you think. They all are, John."

I looked around me, hoping to see a face I knew.

"Gardeners, teachers, guardian angels. All real. All around us."

"And when I die. Someone will lead me home, too? Who will it be?"

"I can't say. I can only promise that as long as there have been men and women to experience mortal life, there has been someone to lead them home. Even your Savior, the Prince of Peace, was led home by a loving, perfect Heavenly Father. There is no room for doubt, John, in His presence. You must accept that *you* are not alone, because *she* is not alone. Willard is not alone either."

"And what of him? Baby Willard? Did my father lead him home, too?"

"He did not. Willard Bevan did not have a Cross Gardener."

I rose to my feet and worked hard to gather my emotions into calm. But I could not. "Why? Did you not just say everyone is led home? Everyone is cared for?"

When he didn't answer me immediately, I took an aggressive step forward. "This *cannot* be." I pointed at him. "This gift of yours, it is *not* real because I *say* it isn't! What of my son? What of Willard? Was he not loved enough?" I could barely collect enough air to finish the sentence.

"I did not say he was not led home, John."

"Then who? How?"

"The One who leads home *all* the children: your Savior."

I began to retreat from the clearing. "How? How do you know all this? The lessons, the details of my life, why you? How? What gives you the privilege of knowing Emma Jane and my son as well as I did?"

He took to his feet and put his hands calmly at his side. "Regardless of the life they lived, their religion, or their age, no one ever, ever leaves this life without an escort waiting for them on the other side of the veil. That same escort then comforts those left behind."

"*This* I understand," I pled, "but how do you know *so much, so young*? Who have *you* led home?"

"I have not led anyone home yet."

"Then who are you? No more games and no more misdirection. How do you know so much?"

He smiled in the most familiar way. "I learned it from you, Dad."

I backed away from the crosses and toward the road. "No."

He took two slow steps toward me.

I retreated. "No, no, you're not. You're a man." I labored. "You're as old as I am." I backed up even farther, stumbling, struggling for balance. "My Willard was a baby. Just a baby."

He continued forward, closing the space between us. "John Bevan, please hear me. They call me a Cross Gardener, but my real name will always be Willard Bevan, son of an orchardist."

"Stop this." The words came with force from my gut. "No, no, no, you're not."

"Yes, I am. You see that I am a man. I am in my prime. I am exactly as you imagine I would have been, aren't I? I have your eyes and chin. My mother's nose. And one day I would have walked and worked the orchard just as you see me now." He stretched his arms out for me.

I backed up even farther until I stepped off the grass and into the loose gravel at the edge of the road.

"Dad, careful!"

I fell backward into the road. A speeding SUV honked and slammed its brakes.

The Cross Gardener walked into the road and extended his hand. "Come."

I put my hand in his. Smooth, unwrinkled, uncut. Warm. I squeezed his hand three times. *I love you.*

He pulled me from the ground and held my hand against his chest. He squeezed it back four times. *I love you, too.*

Thirty-nine
Fair

⚜

L OU Lou loved two things most: animals and cotton candy.

That made the Shenandoah County Fair at the fairgrounds in Woodstock her own street in heaven the last week of every August.

It was August again, and despite the memories I couldn't have talked her out of the fair if our lives depended on it. Honestly, hers might have.

Lou Lou couldn't stop gabbing as we exited in Woodstock. "Can we get chili dogs, Daddy?"

"Sure. But you're riding the Zipper by yourself."

"Do we have time to see the cows, pigs, baby pigs, too? And the chickens and the baby chickens? They better have those bunnies again. Remember how much Mommy loved the bunnies?"

"I sure do."

She sighed. "I miss her, Daddy."

"I miss her, too, Lou Lou. And that's okay." I smiled at her in the rearview mirror and she smiled right back.

We sat in a long line of traffic making its way to Ox Road and the fairground entrance. The rides were already lit and spinning and twirling in the distance.

"First the Ferris wheel, okay, Daddy?"

I hadn't seen a Ferris wheel since Ocean City nine months earlier. "Of course, darling."

"And the swings. Remember last year I still wasn't tall enough for the bumper cars? I will be this year. For sure."

We pulled in and were directed by volunteers in orange vests to the next open spot in the grass parking lot. Lou Lou hopped from the car without Shell and his brown backpack. "He's not coming?"

"Not this year, Daddy."

As we walked through the parking lot I took Lou Lou's hand and squeezed it three times.

She squeezed back four.

We explored every tent, every barn, every display, and petted every animal she could reach, which was almost everything that year. I held her up to the few she couldn't.

Later, while we stood in the line for the slide, Lou Lou asked me just as she had a year before, "Did Grandpa Bevan like the fair just like me?"

"He sure did."

"Did he like the slide?"

"Sure."

"Did he slide in the burlap sack or on his behind?"

"He liked the burlap sack. It made him so fast he also flew right into the air."

"Oh, Daddy, you're a silly sack of apples."

A woman took our tickets, the very same woman who'd taken them a year before. She shared a friendly, Southern smile, oblivious to how important those two burlap sacks in her hand had become.

I said thank you and nearly hugged her.

We hiked up the narrow, slowly rising stairs. From the top, before we sat in our lanes, we could see the picnic table below where Emma Jane had eaten her last dessert, a strawberry funnel cake drowning in whipped cream. I blew a kiss into the air and hoped somewhere, somehow, it found its way to her classroom.

We put our burlap sacks into our lanes and readied for the race below to begin. I looked across the Valley to the north, then turned and looked to the south.

A hot-air balloon hovered high in the distance in the southern part of the Valley.

I wondered what He saw for us.

I also wondered how many Cross Gardeners were working in the Valley that night. If every mourner that day—and every day—would leave an extra white carnation for the Cross Gardeners, the veil might become thinner. Still unseen, but not invisible.

We sped to the bottom of the slide. Laughing. Yelling into the fair air. Lou Lou's brown hair blowing behind her.

Listening.

When dusk turned to black, I carried a tuckered Lou Lou all the way back to my pickup truck. I set her in the backseat and put her seat belt on. When I opened my own door, I ran my hand across the new vinyl lettering: Emma Jane's Orchard.

I looked in the rearview mirror to back up and enter the long path of exiting vehicles.

"Daddy?" Nine months of hard work, hours with counselors, even more hours with me on the orchard—it all rose to the surface and surprised me.

"Yes, darling."

"Can we take the long way home?"

Center Point Publishing
600 Brooks Road ● PO Box 1
Thorndike ME 04986-0001 USA

(207) 568-3717

US & Canada:
1 800 929-9108
www.centerpointlargeprint.com